Temptation

Blue Moon Saloon
Book 2

by Anna Lowe

Twin Moon Press

Editing by Lisa A. Hollett

Covert art by Jacqueline Sweet

Contents

Other books in this series

Blue Moon Saloon

Perfection (a short story prequel)

Damnation (Book 1)

Temptation (Book 2)

Redemption (Book 3)

Salvation (Book 4)

Deception (Book 5)

Celebration (a holiday treat)

visit www.annalowebooks.com

Free Books

Get your free e-books now!

Sign up for my newsletter at *annalowebooks.com* to get three free books!

- *Desert Wolf*: Friend or Foe (Book 1.1 in the Twin Moon Ranch series)

- *Off the Charts* (the prequel to the Serendipity Adventure series)

- *Perfection* (the prequel to the Blue Moon Saloon series)

Chapter One

Cole Harper stood before the swinging saloon doors for a good minute. Maybe two. The sun had set, and the air had that crisp, cool quality it only got in high-altitude Arizona and only on spring evenings, when everything felt fresh and budding and new.

Sounds and smells from the saloon clawed at his shoulders, begging him to come in. Laughter rang out and chairs scraped along the floor. Country music poured from the jukebox, and a couple was starting to dance. The bartender thunked down an empty glass, poured a shot of Jack Daniel's, and slid it all the way down the bar.

All that, he got without looking, just listening. Christ. What was wrong with him?

Go in, already.

Cole kept his thumbs hooked in his jeans and hunched his shoulders, trying to resist the urge.

Scents assaulted him, one after another in a thousand little punches. The peaty scent of aged whiskey, the charcoal flavor of a malt. The mouthwatering smell of spare ribs smoked over mesquite.

His tongue darted out to lick his lips before he could stop it.

Hurry up, already.

He'd been hearing that inner voice for a while now, and it was driving him nuts, like the itch on his arm. He'd been cut two weeks ago — a little bitty cut sustained in a fight in this very saloon, when he'd come along just in time to stop a couple of thugs from jumping the two waitresses. Unbelievably strong guys with weird, clawing nails he'd managed to avoid,

1

except for that one scratch. His skin had healed now, but the itch remained.

An angry growl built in his throat at the memory of the intruders then faded away when he realized the sound was coming from him and not some passing dog.

Jesus, he was growling, now, too?

He coughed it away. Squaring his shoulders, he pushed the saloon's doors wide and marched in, letting them swing behind him. He took off his hat, glanced in the mirror next to the sign that read, *Check your guns at the door,* and ran his fingers through the blond hair that curled and feathered to a point somewhere beneath his ears. Then he headed straight for his chair at the end of the bar. A chair some fool was occupying, which made the growl build in his throat again.

My chair. My spot.

The inner voice was ridiculously territorial. He clenched his fists, telling himself he would not pick a fight. Telling himself it didn't matter who was sitting in which chair.

Except that fool sitting smugly in *his* chair needed to get the hell out. Now.

"Hey, Cole." A voice like honey stopped him, and his head whipped around. And just like that, the tension strung through his body like a thousand-volt current dissipated. The sights and sounds and smells of the saloon faded away, and he was standing in a mountain meadow. It sure felt like that, anyway.

"Hi, Janna," he whispered.

"Hey." She smiled back.

Janna! Janna! The growl turned into a joyous inner cry.

She had her hair in two braids today, a perfect match for her bubbly, little-girl energy. Sometimes she wore it down and let it sway around her face like a liquid frame. Other times, she did this complicated braid thing he dreamed of slowly unraveling and running his fingers through. And sometimes, she just wore a ponytail, and he liked that, too.

He liked everything about Janna. A lot. Her laugh, her smile, her way of tilting her head to listen when he whispered in her ear. He'd liked her since the day he'd first set eyes on the freckled spitfire who'd started waitressing in the saloon not too long ago. Janna always had a sunny smile and sparkling eyes and a chipper voice. Her bouncy step and glossy brown hair were just as full of life as the rest of her. She had a way of looking at him as if she could see *into* him, and she didn't even seem to mind what she found.

He tightened his fingers over his belt and ordered them to stay there. Because *liking* the vivacious waitress had slid right over to *lusting* for her in the past couple of weeks. Like he'd slipped and hit some dial that turned the testosterone up full blast. All he could think of was her. Or rather, him and her. Close. Unbridled. Uncontrolled.

Which didn't make sense. He'd been there, done that with spunky cowgirl-types who could ride and rope and wrangle. What exactly did Janna have that turned on every switch in a burned-out cowboy like him?

Everything. She has everything. She is everything, the inner voice sighed.

When he could think straight, it scared him.

But he couldn't think straight around Janna. She was all the girls he'd ever loved, times fifty. Times a hundred. A thousand. She made him imagine all kinds of crazy things, like standing knee-deep in wildflowers in a meadow in spring. A perfect, peaceful place so unlike the reality that had been haunting him these days. The ceiling fan of the saloon that turned in lazy circles became an eagle, wheeling on a Rocky Mountain breeze. As long as Janna was around, he was in heaven.

He clenched his fists against his sides. He was in the Blue Moon Saloon, damn it. And he was not going crazy. Not yet.

"How are you doing today?" she asked, propping her drink tray against her hip.

Not crazy yet, he nearly said. *But getting closer all the time.* She was the only thing keeping him sane. In the hours he spent alone, he went through the wildest mood swings. One second, he'd be enjoying the scent of leather and horse as he saddled up a ride at the stables where he worked, and the next, he'd be overcome with the bitterest fury, the weirdest urges. Like wanting to run naked at night. Wanting to tip his chin up to the waxing moon hanging over the desert and howl at it. To chase a deer, rip into it with bare teeth, and feast on warm flesh and blood.

"Been good," he fibbed. "How about you?"

A customer walked past, and Janna stepped closer to his side.

God, she smelled nice. Like buttercups and daisies with a trace of forget-me-nots, the blue flowers that were exactly the color of her eyes. All of that blended together in a soothing scent that settled his soul.

Mine. Mate.

He shook his head and looked around, hoping to spot some guy hiding somewhere, throwing his voice. But there was no one. Just the dark, husky voice in his mind that he didn't trust one bit. What was with the mate nonsense, anyway?

"Happy to see you." Janna smiled and tilted forward on the balls of her feet. Just enough that if he wanted, he could kiss her.

It wouldn't be their first kiss, either, because they'd been out dancing a few weeks back, before he'd started losing his mind. It was the first night he'd enjoyed in a long, long time. A great night, even, breathing her in and holding her close and only letting go long enough to whirl her around then pull her straight back into his arms, where he'd whispered in her ear and made her laugh and smile that incredible smile. Fast dancing turned into slow dancing, and slow dancing turned into a melting kind of grind, and the kiss was only the first of many he had planned to shower on her all the way back to his place.

But her friends had interrupted them, and though she'd all but snarled them off, he'd come to his senses and backed away for her own good. He could get drunk on Janna, but she deserved better than him.

Kiss her, the voice growled. *Take her. Mark her!*

He took half a step back. That voice was dangerous. Demanding. Crude. A man didn't *take* from a woman. Not the kind of man he'd been raised to be.

Believe me, she's asking, the voice shot back.

Well, if she was, he had to be the one who kept a clear head. So what if their bodies breezed into a crazy high just from being close?

Need her to survive the Change, the voice inside him murmured. *Need my mate.*

He shivered. Survive? Change? Mate? He truly was losing his mind.

Being around Janna slowed it down, though. She calmed him down. Well, most of the time. Usually, she made him think of a place like that idyllic meadow, where he could lie down with his head in her lap and settle into a profound peace. Sometimes, though, all he could imagine was rolling with her in that meadow. Stripping off her clothes and his and pounding inside her as she wrapped her legs around him and raked her nails across his back. He'd imagine pumping his hips as madly as she'd pump hers while she screamed her pleasure and—

"You okay?" Her brow furrowed.

He took a deep breath and winced at the crushing hardness in his jeans. "Good. Yeah. Great." A lie, but it was better than the truth. *Not okay. Thinking of throwing you over my shoulder and fucking you nowhere near as gently as you deserve.*

Her nostrils flared, and for the briefest of instants, he wondered if she'd like that.

He turned to the bar, trying to clear his mind — only to spot the asshole sitting in his chair again. *His* chair!

He clenched his teeth and his fists, because anger came with an awful, pinching pain under his nails and canines, like they were being pulled out by pliers. Or worse, pushed out from inside to make space for—

"Cole," Janna murmured. The second she put a hand on his arm, the pain faded along with the fury. "I got this."

She scurried ahead and smiled at the man while Cole glared from over her shoulder. Janna was tall, only a couple of inches under his six feet, and she had a self-assured poise that doubled her presence.

"We've got a table for you now," she told the customer, pointing.

5

Cole gritted his teeth and told himself she was smiling at the guy because it was her job, not because the ass deserved it.

"Thanks, sitting at the bar is fine." The man's smile was aimed at Janna, but when his gaze turned to Cole, it faded fast. "On second thought..." He grabbed his drink and fled.

Cole glared at the man's back until Janna stuck an elbow in his ribs, squelching the growl he wasn't aware of until then.

"Look." She patted the barstool and made her voice silky-sweet. "All yours."

Her hand ran over his shoulder, and their eyes met.

All mine, the voice hummed inside.

"All yours." She nodded.

His eyes went wide. Did she really mean...

She steered him onto the stool, and her hands on his waist felt good. Like dancing had been — that feeling of rightness, of belonging, of a perfect fit.

He sat down and she came a little closer. Closer still, like she was getting sucked into the magic spell, too. It took everything he had not to pull her into the space between his legs and deliver a huge, bruising kiss.

"Janna!" the big guy working the bar called. Simon Voss, one of two brothers who ran the place. Well, they pretended to run the place. It was Janna and her sister, the waitresses, who made the place thrive. The brothers were good at security, though, and kept the customers on their best behavior when it came to Janna and Jessica. And Cole was a regular, so they were okay with him, not to mention grateful for his intervention that night of the attack.

Still, Simon shot him a look that said, *Watch it, cowboy. Got my eye on you, too.*

Cole wanted to protest. *Hey, you can trust me!* But he couldn't even trust himself these days, so why should Simon?

Janna pulled away, and his heart ached just at that much space opening up between them. Then she ran a smooth palm over his cheek and whispered, "Be right back," making his soul settle again.

"I'll be right here," he growled as she went. It was a promise and a warning to anyone eyeing her perfect ass. And there were plenty of suspects on that count. A whole saloon full of them, it felt like.

And jeez, the place was hopping tonight. Before Janna and her sister came along, the saloon hadn't pulled in half as many customers. It was listless and dusty and dead — sort of the way he felt. But then Janna had filled it with laughter and smiles and life, and he started coming because. . . because. . .

Well, maybe in spite of himself.

Janna shot him one parting smile over her shoulder, making him go warm all over.

Mine, the inner voice growled. *Mate.*

"I'll be right here," he whispered, telling himself everything would be all right.

Chapter Two

All yours? Janna practically screamed at her inner wolf. *What the hell was that? All yours?*

We're his, the beast hummed back in satisfaction, *and he's ours.*

She cursed under her breath and cut a crooked path through the crowd of customers. Grabbing a full tray of drinks off the far end of the bar, she set off on another round of the saloon.

Stupid wolf. I am not anybody's. I am my own person.

Admit it, her wolf growled. *He's our mate!*

Shhh!

She looked around pensively, as if someone might have overheard that inner exchange. Most of the customers were humans who'd never pick up on it. But another shifter...

She snuck a glance at her sister Jessica, who could usually read her thoughts clear as day. But Jess was busy waiting tables on the other side of the saloon, grinning and glowing the way she'd been ever since she'd won her destined mate — Simon, the bear shifter tending the bar. He hadn't seemed to notice, either, but then, Simon never really noticed anyone but Jess.

Janna let out the breath she'd been holding. Whew. The only other shifters were the four guys in the corner, strapping young wolves from Twin Moon Ranch, and they were too busy talking shop to pick up on the inner dialogue of a love-sick she-wolf.

"Draft?" She held up a glass.

"Mine," one of the ranch hands lifted a finger.

"Wild Turkey?"

"Over here," a second said.

"Jim Beam?"

"Mine," the third man said.

Her gaze wandered across the saloon to Cole, and her wolf growled.

Mine.

She ground her teeth together behind the smile she plastered on top. "Anything else I can get you?"

"That's it, thanks."

She dropped off another couple of drinks at table four, checked in on the neighboring group, and cleared plates from table seven. Cole's storm-cloud eyes tracked her the whole time. His gaze pressed on her like a physical thing. Like a blanket, thrown over her shoulders on a winter's night in Montana.

Except she wasn't in Montana anymore, and it sure as hell wasn't winter.

Told you. He's our mate.

She shook her head. How could the beast be so sure? God knew she'd gotten love and lust mixed up in the past. But this felt different. Spine-tingling different. Lightning-sparks-in-the-veins different.

My destined mate, her wolf growled.

It sure felt like it. But one thing didn't fit. Destined mates were supposed to recognize each other on first sight. And she'd gone two whole weeks simply liking Cole. Okay, *really* liking Cole. Badly-wanting-to-tango-on-the-nearest-horizontal-surface kind of liking Cole. But there hadn't been that instant connection of souls. That, *Bang! Your life will never be the same* revelation that mated shifters talked about.

Her attraction to him snuck up on her steadily ever since... since... well, since some point she couldn't quite put her finger on, and then — *whoosh!* Her vague crush on Cole went to all-out desire. A day and night craving. A need that scared her.

Mate. My destined mate, her wolf cooed.

But wolves, as every female shifter knew, were not to be trusted. Not in matters of the heart.

Probably she was just crushing on Cole. Really, really badly. The man was hot as sin and an amazing dancer to boot. A charmer with a crooked, boyish grin. A man she could talk to every night for hours about the same thing and never get tired of what he had to say, or how he said it.

Yep. Just a crush. She'd get over it in, um—

Another two or three hundred years? her wolf snorted.

She was so wrapped up in arguing with her wolf that she worked on autopilot — and whoops, without even realizing it, she had headed his way with a plate of key lime pie she was supposed to be delivering to another customer. God, what was she doing?

"Got just what you need." She smiled and set the plate in front of him.

Her heart beat a little faster, seeing the little-boy grin spread on his face. One of the many Cole quirks she'd fallen in love with over the past couple of weeks. One second, he'd be all broody warrior, harboring some deep, dark wound she was dying to heal. But just as quickly, the lines around his mouth would fall away and he'd be a kid again, all twinkling eyes and aw-shucks country charm.

"My favorite," he murmured, as he did with anything she brought him.

His scrappy blond hair curled just below his ears. Fine, golden strands that waved this way and that. So, so tempting to run her fingers through. His full lips quivered the slightest bit, and she had to bite her own to resist reaching for his.

Mate, her wolf sighed.

She forced herself not to bat her eyelashes or pucker her lips. Not to do anything that gave her — lust? love? — away. But her nipples kept standing up, and the scent wafting off her shoulders was the sticky-sweet fragrance of arousal.

Janna.

Her head whipped around, and the goofy love music playing in her mind broke off with the screech of a needle ripping across an old-fashioned LP.

Soren was calling to her from over by the bar. The bigger of the two bear brothers stood with his beefy arms folded over his chest, glowering. The very picture of a clan alpha. A none-too-pleased clan alpha, nodding her toward the back of the saloon.

Shit, shit, shit. Someone had noticed her fawning over Cole, after all.

Cole's eyes followed hers, and she darted into his line of sight, because the last thing she needed was for a headstrong cowboy to get into a glaring contest with her two-hundred-pounds-of-solid-muscle boss. Cole might be made of the roughest, toughest stuff, but he was still human, despite the growl building in his throat.

Wait, a growl? Her head whipped back to Cole.

She smoothed a hand over his chest without thinking, and the noise stopped. Everything stopped for a moment, and the whole world ceased to exist. Zoomed a million miles away, in fact, until all that remained was the sensation of little licking flames passing between their bodies. Telling her to step closer. Closer. . .

She tilted her head and focused on those incredibly kissable lips. Sniffed his cool, clean scent. Rose to the balls of her feet—

Janna! Soren barked, and the world came crashing back. Glass clinked against glass. The bassline of a Johnny Cash song thumped from the jukebox. A dozen voices chattered. Soren glared.

She broke away from Cole, blinking. "Gotta get to work."

Mate! her wolf wailed as she forced one foot in front of another and followed Soren to the back room of the saloon. Away from Cole. Away from the cheery action. Away from the crowd.

Shit, shit, shit.

Soren stomped into the dim back room and loomed over her.

"Janna."

"Soren." She stuck her chin up and crossed her arms much as he'd just done. Two could play at that game. His big, bad alpha act wasn't all act, but Soren was more of an older brother to her than boss.

"A human?" Soren's eyebrows were darker than his sandy brown hair, and when he lifted the one on the right...

"You look just like your grandfather when you do that," she said, catching him off guard. Catching herself off guard, too, because the gesture had snapped her back in time, to when she was a young member of the wolfpack and neighbor to his bear clan in Montana. Soren was a good ten years older than her, the man being groomed to take over the clan one day.

"I mean, a younger version of your grandfather," she squeaked.

He grimaced, but a shine of pride lit his eyes. The two of them didn't have much in common, but they both shared that soft spot for memories of home and the loved ones they'd lost.

Soren's gaze went from sentimental to distant and even bitter, so she put a hand on his arm.

"It was good that you weren't in Montana when it happened," she whispered.

He growled at the floorboards, but his shoulders sagged at the mention of *it* – the attack that had annihilated both their packs.

About the only thing that could defeat a man like Soren was that feeling of failure. That alpha pride, that *I should have been there to defend my clan* loyalty. It would haunt him for the rest of his life.

A roar of laughter sounded from the saloon, and Soren's growl went back to one of displeasure.

"You know better than to mess with a human," he said.

She clenched her fists and beat back her wolf before it started crowing about mates and love and forever. Cole was just a crush, right?

An all-consuming, all-encompassing crush.

Soren looked toward the front room. "Simon and Jess, they need to be together. Destiny wants that." His expression went from glad for his brother to mournful. Soren had had a destined mate, too, but she'd been murdered in the rogue attack along with everyone else. "But we have to watch out."

Her chin snapped up. "You think they'll be back?"

They, of course, were the rogues who'd ambushed her and Jess a few weeks ago. The same rogues who had wiped out her pack and Soren's bear clan months ago in a surprise attack.

"Fucking purists," Soren spat one of his rare curses. The rogues were part of a movement that called for racial purity among shifters. No wolves mixing with bears, and certainly no mixing with humans. The hard-liners exercised their own brand of terror and vigilante justice.

Janna shivered, thinking of the inferno Jess had pulled her from in Montana, and more recently, the half-dozen rogues who'd appeared in the saloon.

"If we give them reason to come back..." Soren's eyes traveled toward the front room, and the message was clear. Janna flirting with a human could attract another rogue ambush. The rogues would plan their attack more carefully next time, but they'd be back.

Her wolf snarled inside. *No one will keep me from my mate!*

Not my mate, she insisted. *Just a whole lot of trouble.*

Mate! Her wolf chanted. *Mate!*

"Look, Cole is a good guy, but he's not one of us," Soren said. "We have to protect what we have here. What we're building here."

She could see it in his eyes: the vision of a new clan. A fair and stable clan — or pack or whatever they decided to call their unusual mishmash of bears and wolves. A clan risen from the ashes of what they'd lost in Montana. One in which it didn't matter what type of shifter you were as long as you worked hard and played by the rules.

Rules that said you had to be a shifter and not human. Janna hung her head. He was right.

Soren gave her a last stern look, then tilted his head toward the door in a weary gesture.

"Back to work," he murmured, then gave her a tired smile. "Both of us."

She studied him for a moment, wondering why she felt pity for the mighty bear.

Mighty, but broken, like Simon once was, her wolf decided.

No wonder she felt pity. Simon and Jess had found their happiness, and she had her whole life ahead of her, too. But Soren faced a long and lonely existence without his destined mate.

A whole life ahead of us, her wolf agreed, conjuring up an image of Cole.

She strode back into the saloon faster than she'd intended, and her head went right to Cole's spot at the end of the bar. Now more than ever, she needed the reassurance that he was there. Just one look, one strand of hope. One moment of connection.

She craned her neck past customers, then took another step. Cole's chair was empty. Her heart stuttered when she saw the saloon doors swinging on their hinges.

He'd left? Already?

Her nostrils flared, tracking his scent. And just like that, her wolf took over and made her race out the door.

Mate! Don't go!

It was all she could do not to blurt it out loud as she scanned the sidewalk to her left and right. Quiet. Deserted, except for a couple walking across the street.

That way! Her wolf pushed her to the left, following his scent. She ran down the sidewalk, turned a sharp corner, and spotted a tall figure approaching a pickup.

"Cole!" That time, she did say it out loud. When he spun around, her whole soul sang. *Mine! Mate!*

"Cole," she panted, catching up at last. All but plowing him over in her haste to... to... to what, exactly, she had no clue. Only that she wasn't ready to let him go. Not so soon, and not without a word, a parting touch.

His arms came up just as hers did, and they stood there for a second, gripping each other by the forearms like a couple of trapeze artists getting ready to jump. His dark eyes were lit with pinpoints of light, a universe that sucked her right in on a magical ride.

"Um... uh..." she mumbled, lost for words.

"You okay?"

His voice was shaky, so she boomeranged the question back. "Yeah. You?"

He nodded, and a tiny grin opened on his face. He didn't seem okay, not by a long shot, but he was glad to see her. As glad as she was to see him, it seemed.

She slid her arms up to his shoulders — ridiculously boxy shoulders she could barely get a grip on — and grinned right back. "Leaving already?"

He pinched his lips together for a moment and closed his eyes. "Don't want to go, but..."

She searched his face. But, what? What exactly was wrong?

His cheek twitched, and when he opened his eyes, he scanned the sky before looking at her.

"I have to. I have to go."

She wanted to shake him and ask why, but his eyes begged her not to.

"Cole..." She ran her thumb along his collarbone, wishing she could ease whatever weighed so heavily on his mind. But Cole was like the Voss brothers in many ways; talking would only make him as grumbly as a bear.

"Gotta go." He whispered, and his voice cracked as if he really, really didn't want any such thing.

Must help our mate! her wolf whimpered inside.

Easier said than done, because how could she help a man who refused any help?

Her father had been like that, too. A pack alpha who tried to solve every problem on his own. But her mother had found a remedy for that. She'd countered darkness with light. With hope. With love.

Her wolf wagged its tail. *Love. Hope. Light.*

She leaned in to Cole, not just touching him but warming him with her body. Smiling at him, because nothing was more important than finding something to smile about in life. She slid her arms behind his shoulders and tipped her chin up, just as she had when he'd first walked into the saloon.

"Can't have you leave without saying goodbye," she murmured, then eased into a kiss. Slowly, carefully, in case he

16

decided to bolt. Stroking his back gently, willing the tension away.

His lips met hers eagerly. Tenderly, as if he were afraid of hurting her. His chest rose and fell on a silent sigh, and she smiled against his lips. Yep, a kiss was just what her brooding cowboy needed tonight. Her delicious, quivering cowboy, who smelled of pine and mountain air and mustang, wild and free.

Her wolf was all for diving deeper into that kiss, but she fought back the urge. He didn't need fire and passion right now. He needed an anchor. A light to guide him through whatever thorny maze he'd lost himself in.

So she packed light and hope and happiness into her kiss, communicating in tiny lifts and pulls of her lips. The night was cool and fresh. The streets quiet, the stars bright. She had her man, her mate. She could make this minute last forever if she believed in it hard enough.

Forever, her wolf hummed deep inside.

She coaxed the tension out of him, one strand of muscle at a time. Her hands warmed his neck, then rubbed his shoulders. Stroked his back the way she might stroke a dog still bristling after a fight. Pressed her chest against his and counted heavy heartbeats. Counted double sometimes, because hers got mixed up with his.

They might have gone hours pressed together like that, all through the night and halfway through the sunrise that was sure to come galloping in on its heels, but a car drove down a side street with the radio thumping loud.

She broke off the kiss but not the contact. Turning her ear to his shoulder, she rested her head, listening to the tune fade down the street.

"We really need to go dancing again sometime, cowboy," she sighed. Her body tingled just remembering the moves he'd swept her through, the way he'd whispered in her ear.

His arms tightened around her, and he nodded into her hair.

"That, we do."

"Promise?" Her voice rose in hope.

"Promise," he rumbled, and his low tone vibrated through her chest, warming her another couple of degrees.

They stood for another minute like that, and she fantasized about hanging on even longer. But before some other reminder of the outside world slammed into their bubble of perfection, she eased away, letting the magic seal around Cole. Let him hang on to that serenity as long as he could. Let him drive home and sleep well and rest his weary soul.

"See you tomorrow?" she asked, sliding her hands back to his forearms. Back to that feeling of a trapeze artist — this time, coming to rest after an amazing feat.

And it was amazing, because Cole smiled, and the stars showered her with silent applause. She'd done it.

"See you tomorrow." He nodded, locking his eyes on hers.

"Promise?" she added, teasing a little now.

"Promise."

Chapter Three

Cole put his pickup in gear and drove off, still savoring her kiss, still tingling from her touch. His eyes were tempted to stray to the rearview mirror, but he forced them to stay on the road. He clenched his hands around the steering wheel and told himself it was better not to look. Janna had pulled him back from the edge of a cliff with her taste of heaven, and now it was time to go.

He half expected the inner voice to pipe up, screaming something like, *Go back! Take her with us!* But it was mercifully silent for a change. Well, not entirely silent, because if he really listened, he could hear a sleepy, satisfied purr.

He threw the pickup into another gear and stepped on the gas. God, he really was going nuts. The mood swings had been getting worse and worse. He'd gone from flying high when he'd first seen Janna in the saloon to choking on jealousy when Soren had called her to the back room. The second she was out of sight, a fever had started up. An uncontrollable fury and possessiveness.

Get her back! She's ours! Ours!

He'd been *that* close to following them, because it was all too reminiscent of the day she'd been attacked. The day some sixth sense had told him to stop by the saloon after hours, just in case. To follow the angry voices coming from the back room where he'd found Janna and her sister cornered by five big guys. One of the sisters had been holding a stool up in self-defense, the other, a broken-off bottle. Both of them looking more defiant than scared and absolutely ready to fight.

The room had practically been humming with some kind of weird static electricity, too. Something angry and animalistic, like a bull waiting to be released from a pen. The second he'd walked in, he knew he'd be in for a hell of a fight.

That was weeks ago. Tonight, every inner alarm in his body rang when Janna followed Soren out of sight. Which made no sense. Soren was a good man who'd never hurt her. Janna shared the apartment above the saloon with him and their siblings, for Christ's sake!

Maybe that's why he'd started resenting the guy so much.

She's ours, not his! the voice had screamed when she'd stepped out of sight.

He wanted to shrug the feeling off and say that Janna wasn't his, and she wasn't Soren's, either. But he couldn't quite get himself to say the words. Even if Soren wasn't involved with Janna beyond being a housemate, the man exuded a stallion's kind of cool arrogance as he watched over his herd. His whole stance screamed, *Mine! I guard them. I care for them. Mine!*

Which was good, in a way, because it kept a saloon full of potential rowdies in line. Soren made damn sure the customers didn't dare get any bad ideas when it came to the waitresses.

Cole cursed. *He* was the one getting bad ideas — like stomping down the hallway to see what was going on. Like standing half a step behind Janna and glaring down Soren as if the saloon manager were the trespasser and not the other way around.

One minute longer in the saloon, and he just might have lost control, so he'd taken off. Headed for his truck with the same urge for motion that had made him come to Arizona in the first place.

But then Janna had caught up with him and restored the peace and balance in him again. Kissed him just long and hard enough to turn the lights in his soul back on.

He drove, replaying the kiss over and over in his mind, because thinking about it kept him swimming in a sea of serenity instead of buffeted by a storm.

He drove ten miles west, to where the dense lights of town spread farther and farther apart. Glanced up at a sky full of stars and looked around. Ducked his head to check every possible angle and only relaxed his grip on the wheel when he was sure the moon wasn't visible on the horizon.

He worked his shoulders in loose circles. No moon was good. No moon meant he had half a chance of getting through the night sane.

When he made it home and parked, he shut the car door quietly, not wishing to disturb the fragile peace he felt. Then he snuck up to his apartment over the barn and hopped straight into bed like a kid trying not to get caught for staying out too late.

And miracle of miracles, he actually got to sleep. A deep, restful sleep — the kind he remembered from a long time ago. The only dreams that flitted across his brain were good ones, full of meadows and flowers and gurgling mountain streams. Some of the dreams, he ambled through alone, and in others — the best ones — he had Janna at his side and her hand firmly clasped in his. A few were a little weird, with wildflowers springing up against his nose and tickling his belly because he was crouched over them on all fours. Make that four feet and a tail that wouldn't stop wagging because Janna was there, too. Her body was hidden by the tall grass, and she seemed to have shrunk, too, but he could smell her, right in front of him. And that was nice. Calming. Peaceful.

And yeah, weird, but whatever. He'd take what he could get.

He woke up sometime in the middle of the night and blinked for a while, feeling unusually good for a change. No booze drumming through his head. No nightmares itching through his bones. No memories haunting him.

He wandered over to the bathroom, half asleep, then headed back to bed, hoping for more sleep. But when his gaze strayed out the window, his blood ran cold.

The moon. A fat, greedy, almost-full moon, shining right into his apartment. Right on him like a spotlight, saying, *I want you. I control you.*

He yanked the flimsy curtains together, flopped back on the bed, and turned his back to the window. Pretended he couldn't feel the pull of the moon on his body. Somewhere on the Earth, the ocean was being drawn into a high tide by that force, and for the first time ever, he felt the tug of it, too. On his skin. On his blood. On his soul.

No matter how much he willed the dreams of Janna back, all he got were nightmares. The moon pulled on him like a puppet that twisted and jolted and jumped. He observed it from the outside, though he was still connected enough to feel the pain. The moon pulled him apart, limb from limb, then reassembled the pieces in the wrong way.

Then the nightmare had him running. He was furious. Dangerous. Foaming at the mouth. Chasing some helpless prey over wooded hills. Closing in for the kill and getting absolutely, uncontrollably high from the adrenaline of it. He ripped a doe apart with teeth that couldn't be his and relished the bitter taste of hot blood dripping down his chin. Wolves appeared to try to steal a piece, and he snapped and growled, chasing them off. A couple of sad-eyed bears came along, too, shaking their heads at him, and when they wandered on without getting involved, his soul cried.

Lost cause, one of the bears muttered to the other.

Not worth our time, the second one agreed.

And then his heart stopped, because Janna appeared behind the bears, looking at him. Bright and beautiful as ever except for the disgust written all over her face.

Not worth my time, she said and loped off behind the bears.

Help me! He wanted to scream to them. *Don't give up on me!*

"Give up..." he yelped into the darkness, jolting upright in a cold sweat. The arm he threw out knocked the light off the bedside table, and glass shattered across the floor. The shards glimmered eerily in the moonlight seeping through the curtain.

He panted into the sheets for a while, then stumbled to the bathroom to splash water over his face. He scrubbed his eyes and stared in the mirror, scared as hell at what he might do next. Put his fist through a wall? Howl at the moon?

Find her. Find my mate, the voice growled inside.

He backed away from the mirror. Locked the door he never bothered locking and put a chair in front of it — not to keep anyone out, but to keep himself in, because the images that came with the voice were ugly. He saw Janna, screaming frantically. Fighting off insistent hands that grabbed at places no man had a right to touch, not when a woman didn't want him to.

Janna, fighting *him* madly. It was him in that vision, forcing her.

"No!" He yelled it out loud, and the vision wavered.

He shook his head, swearing he'd never, ever hurt her. That wouldn't, couldn't ever be him.

Just a dream, just a dream...

But, shit. What were those crazy ideas doing in his head, anyway? If he was capable of imagining such things, maybe he was capable of doing them, too.

"Never," he grunted at the ceiling. "Never."

He said it a hundred times, then another hundred, and another. Eventually, he drifted through an uneasy half slumber until he blinked at a shaft of sunlight knifing through the room. Tilted his head at the sound of a rooster crowing outside.

He glanced at the clock. Almost six a.m. Sunrise.

The rooster crowed again. *Get moving, you ass!*

He rolled out of bed and crunched right past the shattered glass of the lamp in bare feet. He paid the little cuts and spikes of pain no heed as he stared into the bathroom mirror. The face he found there was a stranger who looked a lot like him, but not like the him he remembered. This one was darker. Messier. Crazier. He could see it in the eyes.

Jesus, man, he wanted to say. *Who are you?*

Not the Cole Harper he used to be. The one who could smile and flirt and joke. The one who could focus on anything he wanted and go after it with single-minded determination. The one who wasn't scared of anything. Not bucking broncs or the bulls he'd ridden or the ones he'd faced down when he went from bull riding to bullfighting — not clowning, some called it, though saving the life of a fallen rider was anything but — because that gave him an even bigger high. *Real* bullfighting —

not that gory stuff they did in Spain with capes and who knew what. Bullfighting, as in rodeo bullfighting — going face-to-face with raging beasts looking to trample the cowboys they'd just bucked off. That's what he used to do — save those men's lives.

And nothing had ever stopped him. Nothing ever made him give up. Until...

Until one day that started perfectly and quickly went to hell in a real-life nightmare that was worse than anything his imagination could conjure up.

He splashed again and watched the water trickle slowly down his face.

Crap, was he messed up.

So get yourself back together, the growl in his head said. *Win my mate!*

If the voice had come with a face, he'd have punched it out the window of his apartment and right into the water trough downstairs. What the hell was that voice?

He stood in the shower, trying to figure it out. Maybe the pain killers he'd tried taking for a while were mixing with the alcohol he'd been drowning himself in over the past couple of months. Some kind of delayed reaction that was messing with his mind.

Except the voice has been getting worse, asshole, he told himself. *Even though you've been drinking less.*

He paused on that thought. He had been drinking less ever since he'd met Janna. Didn't have much choice, what with her sneaky tricks.

"Your whiskey." She'd wink and set down a glass filled with Coke. Then she'd smile at him with eyes so full of hope and innocence and belief — *belief*, damn it, like she was so sure of him — that he'd had no choice but to gulp the Coke down. Gulp it and smack his lips and joke to the burly bartender that the saloon really ought to stock stronger stuff.

Simon would roll his eyes at Janna's misplaced crusade and go right back to watching her sister's every move with his love-struck, faithful eyes.

Cole thought back in time. Thought forward. Tried to match things up. The inner voice started after he'd slowed the drinking down. Sometime after he'd been knocked out in that fight at the saloon, that time he'd walked in on the men who'd cornered Janna and Jess.

Maybe that was it. His brain had gotten rattled when he'd been thrown against the wall. The guy he'd been grappling with seemed to possess superhuman strength. But shit, he'd had a couple of other falls in his life that had knocked him cold, and none of them left him imagining voices in his head.

Christ, maybe he ought to go back to drinking again.

No way, the voice shot back. *Must please our mate, and she doesn't like it.*

He got out of the shower, finger-combed his hair, and risked another glance in the mirror. He looked gloomy. And tired. So, so tired.

He made himself the world's strongest coffee and a burned piece of toast then headed down the creaky outside stairs to the barn. Slowly, to soak in the sunlight, which reminded him of Janna and everything good.

"Heya, Pip." He tossed his toast crust to the one-eyed Chihuahua-pit bull mix that came running up to him with its tail wagging as it did every day.

The dog scrambled to a halt, though, then backed away.

"Hey!" he protested, stepping closer.

Pip skittered back, showing his teeth.

"Hey, what did I do?" he called after the dog. Then he kicked the dirt. "Great." The only two souls in the world who looked at him without judgment were Pip and Janna, and now Pip hated him.

Which only left Janna. And Christ, how long would it be before she gave up on him, too?

"Bad night, Cole?" Rosalind called to him from a few stalls down.

Ros was old enough to be his grandmother and fussed over him like one, too. The indomitable Annie Oakley-type owned Lazy Q Stables and pretty much ran the place on her own, but she said she liked having a man around. Still, Cole suspected the job was more about her taking care of him than him taking care of the horses. She tut-tutted over how much or how little he ate, drank, and slept, as if she'd lost track of how many sons she'd given birth to and had taken Cole under her wing. Him and Pip and half a dozen horses everyone else had given up on as too old or too creaky or too jittery to be of much use.

No wonder he'd always felt at home in this place.

"Morning, Ros," he sighed, grabbing a saddle. "How many today?"

The trail ride business in this part of Arizona had more downs than ups, but Rosalind usually managed to rustle up just enough customers to pay the bills.

"Eight riders," she said, filling a bucket with oats. "You can start with Dakota, then saddle up Rye. . ."

He set the saddle along a rail and strode into Dakota's stall, thankful for this bit of normalcy. Having grown up on a ranch, he could do this job in his sleep. Saddle a couple of horses, clean the stalls. A dead-end job he'd have scoffed at a year ago, but hell, it worked for him now. It earned him a bit of cash and came with the two-room apartment above the stables. Perfect for a not-too-picky wash-up of a cowboy trying to escape the ghosts of his past.

The job had also come without any questions asked about why a guy in his prime would want an end-of-the-road job at a dusty stable that barely made ends meet, as long as he knew horses. And he knew horses, all right. Horses and bulls.

"Morning, Dakota," he murmured, stepping inside the stall.

The pinto nickered once in greeting, but then her ears went from flopping drowsily to folded back in alarm, and she sidestepped away.

"Whoa, there," he tried, keeping his voice low.

The horse huffed. Her pink nostrils opened wide, testing the air. She pawed at the hay under her feet.

"Come on, just a little trail ride." He clipped the lead on to her halter on the third try. God, why was the horse so jittery?

She pranced around as he led her out and tossed her head restlessly the whole time he saddled her. The mare only really settled down once he'd led her outside and left her tied to a post, ready to ride.

Damn horse. Maybe she'd had a bad night, too.

But horse after horse acted the same way, and even Rosalind shook her head at him.

"What's with you, boy?"

Shit. He wished he knew.

"Whatever it is that's eating at you, keep it out of the barn. Last thing I need is jittery horses with guests who can barely tell a horse's head from its ass." She stepped closer and took his chin in her hand. Turned his head right, then left, the way she studied sick horses and cows. "That girl of yours turn you down?"

"Girl?" How would Rosalind know about Janna? And Janna hadn't turned him down. Not yet, anyway.

She chuckled. "Whatever poor girl who's been working so hard at cleaning you up."

He stepped back, running a hand over his chin. The stubble felt strange, because he usually shaved. Well, over the past couple of weeks, at least, so Janna wouldn't think he was a complete bum.

Rosalind smacked him on the shoulder. "Seems like a girl worth keeping, if you ask me."

He hadn't, but that wouldn't stop Ros.

"A girl worth trying a little harder for," she went on, looking at him with that *Son, I expect better from you* look.

A girl worth dying for, the voice in his head added with a growl.

"Um..." he tried. What exactly did a man say to that? *A girl who deserves better than me?*

Ros smacked his other shoulder, hard enough to make him shuffle. "Back to work. Quit upsetting the horses. And tonight..." Her wrinkled face took on a mischievous glow. "Tonight, you get some flowers and bring them to her, and..." She winked, then cleared her throat. "And I'm sure you can figure it out from there."

Cole leaned against the barn door, watching Rosalind breeze outside like a whirling dervish honing in on a new target. He wanted to protest because he hadn't done anything to piss Janna off.

Haven't done anything to earn her, either, a grouchy voice said.

He considered that. Wondered what to do. Wondered if he trusted himself to do it. His eyes drifted over the pine-dotted hills, then stopped at the crest of the ridge. The pale moon was just starting to slide behind it, setting in the morning light. Wouldn't be long until the moon would be full, rising and setting opposite the sun.

Need her, the voice inside him turned grave. *Need her to survive the Change...*

He fought off a shiver that had no right shaking anyone's shoulders on a warm Arizona day and headed back into the barn.

Chapter Four

Janna rubbed her eyes and yawned as she padded down the stairs to the saloon, wishing she'd had the kind of night she'd dreamed about — up close and personal with Cole Harper — instead of just another lonely night alone.

"Morning," Soren grumbled from the tiny office off the back room of the saloon.

Bears were about as enthusiastic about mornings as she was. The only one of the shifters living above the Blue Moon Saloon who didn't mind waking before ten was her sister, Jessica. The proof was in the smell of fresh muffins wafting over from the little café next door.

"Muffin?" she asked, starting toward the back door.

Soren nodded. "Coffee?"

It had become an amiable ritual between them: he'd get the coffee, she'd get the muffins, and they'd both get on with whatever business there was to be done that day before opening the saloon.

She walked outside and looped from the rear door of the saloon to the back door of the café.

"Morning!" Jessica practically sang when Janna came in.

"Morning," she mumbled back, suppressing a sigh. Her sister had always been a morning person, but the joyous glow she'd taken on recently made it that much harder to bear.

Jessica held up a rack of steaming muffins. "Blackberry-currant. You think Simon will like them?"

Simon's deep voice rumbled from the open door. "I like everything you make." He stood in the doorway, rubbing a shoulder against the frame, marking his turf.

Jessica turned an even happier shade of pink and rushed into his hug.

Janna looked at the floor. Sighed. Grabbed three muffins — one for her, two for Soren — and headed past the happy lovers. She was glad for her sister and Simon, but there was only so much cooing and hand-feeding of muffins an innocent bystander could take.

"Muffin," she sighed, plonking the plate in front of Soren.

"Coffee," he yawned, handing her a mug.

They stood there sipping for a second, listening to the giggling next door, staring off into space. Janna had never been big on the concept of destined mates, figuring she could damn well choose her own partner if she ever decided she wanted one. But seeing Simon and Jess made her think twice. And ever since she'd met Cole...

Mate. Her wolf nodded happily. *Mine.*

Soren took a bear-sized bite of muffin then sighed at the papers littering his desk. The guy loved woodwork, spare ribs, and rooting around in the outdoors. A bear doing office work, well, it just wasn't natural.

Janna took hold of the back of his chair and spun him around. "How about you go for a morning walk. I'll take care of the bills."

His listless eyes lit up a little and turned toward the hills. A hint of oaky bear scent wafted off him, just from the thought of shifting.

"Um... well..."

"Just go." She jerked her thumb at the door. "I got this."

"Maybe just a short walk..."

She pushed him toward the door. Well, she shoved at his broad back, because bears didn't budge unless they damn well wanted to. Obviously, his bear was all for it, because he was out the door, in his pickup, and off on the ten-minute drive to the national forest before she could say boo.

"Boo," she whispered, looking at the sea of paperwork. She took one more sip of coffee and dug into the bills piled up on the desk.

Power, water, deliveries. She slit open envelopes, wrote checks, and made notes in the old-fashioned ledger that was Soren's attempt at office organization.

Rent. She signed that check with a happy face in the memo line, because Tina Hawthorne-Rivera would be the one cashing it. If it weren't for Tina, Simon and Soren might not have managed to rent the saloon from the wolves of Twin Moon Ranch. If it weren't for Tina, Janna might still be on the run with Jessica, working temporary jobs with one eye over her shoulder and one eye on the road. If it weren't for Tina, a lot of good things might never have come to pass.

Like her job here at the saloon. Her cozy room upstairs. Like meeting Cole.

It wasn't Tina, a little voice in the back of her mind said. *It was destiny.*

She mulled that one over as she checked the next envelope. No return address, no logo. Her heart beat a little faster, and she cast a furtive glance at the door.

Probably it's from the new microbrewery in Flagstaff, she told herself, trying not to tremble as she opened it up. *Or maybe an appeal for a local charity. Or maybe—*

She pulled the letter out and stared at the three lines of text.

Purity! Purity! the top line proclaimed in bold.

Tainted shifters shall pay with their lives came under that, and at the bottom. . .

Her stomach lurched.

You will pay with your lives.

The *you* was underlined four times, as it always was.

She crumpled the letter and threw it in the trash. Brushed her hands like she'd just handled a dead rat, then reached into the trash and pushed the letter even deeper. She glanced at the door, making sure no one was there to see. Then she forced herself to reach for the next bill and open it as if nothing had happened. As if the evil that hunted her was watching for her reaction on a hidden camera.

She sat ramrod straight and went through another three bills, pretending to be cool and calm. But inside, her gut churned.

The Blue Bloods hadn't given up their hateful campaign. She was still a target. She and Jess both, plus Simon and Soren. All because their wolf and bear packs had mingled too closely for the shifter extremists who valued racial purity above all else. The Blue Bloods had ambushed the bear clan, then attacked her pack.

She stared into empty space and remembered the flames. The screams. Remembered Jessica yelling at her to run for her life. They'd gotten away, the sole survivors of that awful night.

Survivors of another awful night, too, not too long ago. The Blue Bloods had hunted her and Jessica right to the Blue Moon Saloon, and if it hadn't been for Cole stepping in, then Simon and Soren arriving just when she'd given up hope, she would have been dead.

We'll be back...

She could hear the taunting cry of Victor Whyte, the leader of the Blue Blood rogues as he escaped out the back door of the saloon.

She glanced at the trash can. Were the letters a precursor to more trouble, or were the Blue Bloods all bark and no bite?

"Gotcha, baby." Simon's teasing voice meandered in from next door as he flirted with his mate.

Janna rolled her shoulders and told herself to relax. There was no need to worry. She had two bears around, plus the protection of the Twin Moon wolves — the most powerful pack in the Southwest. The Blue Bloods wouldn't dare stage another attack on the saloon. Would they?

She shook her head vehemently. There was no point living in fear, just like there was no point constantly mourning everything she'd lost in Montana. She was an upbeat, glass half-full type. She had to be because, otherwise, she might just grow old and bitter and spend her days sighing over a long list of regrets.

"Hey, Janna!" her sister called, and she practically jumped out of the chair.

"Yes?"

"Do you want to try my new muffin recipe?"

"Be right there." She pushed away from the desk, happy to escape those thoughts for a while. She'd debated telling the others about the letters but decided against it. They all knew the Blue Bloods were out there. But the rogues had been taught a lesson, and they wouldn't come wandering around here again.

All bark and no bite. She let the sentiment echo in her mind as she stepped out of the tiny office and looked around the back room of the saloon. She and Jess had fought off the Blue Bloods there, and Cole had come along at just the right time. He'd fought like a champion, too, until the rogues threw him against a wall. She closed her eyes, replaying that awful moment when he'd crashed and gone limp. Remembered shaking him and sobbing when he didn't come to. Expecting the worst. But he'd been all right in the end. He'd shaken himself back to his senses and came out of the fight without a scratch.

Without a scratch...

Her mind stuck on that thought as she stared at the wall he'd been thrown against.

All bark and no bite...

"Janna!" Jess called, pulling her onward.

"Have fun." Simon smiled as they crossed paths outside.

Bark... bite... scratch... Her stomach tightened as she thought it through.

"Try this." Jess held out a muffin as she entered the café through the rear door. "Blueberry supreme. Simon's new favorite."

Janna nibbled but barely registered the taste. She helped her sister in the kitchen, because opening day for the new café was only two weeks away, and Jessica was working on some new recipes. It took two hours for Janna to work up the nerve to bring up what was on her mind.

"Jess..." she asked, gulping it down. "Have you noticed anything about... well, about Cole?"

Her sister chuckled. "You mean other than the fact that half the women in the saloon bat their eyes every time he walks in?"

"I mean... Well, anything else?"

"You mean, other than the fact that he looks at you like the sun might fade forever if you step out of the room? Other than the fact that he's like a love-struck puppy around you?"

Janna faked a laugh to match her sister's.

Love-struck puppy or love-struck wolf?

"He has been moody lately," Jess added in a more serious afterthought. "But then, that man's always had something eating at him."

Cole had been awfully moody for the past few weeks. Mercurial, like spring weather back in Montana. He'd go from a dreamy kind of calm to sheer volcanic rumble in two seconds flat, and his gray eyes would go from darting restlessly around to calm as a fair weather cloud, drifting easily in a breeze.

On a razor's edge, in other words.

Shit, shit, shit.

Jess shrugged and went back to washing a bowl. "Poor man's probably going through withdrawal, now that you've gotten him to quit the hard drinking."

Part of her wanted to swell with pride, because it was partially true. She'd been steadily working down his alcohol intake, and it had worked.

But a sinking feeling in her gut told her that wasn't the reason for his mood swings. The real reason could be something else. Something terrible.

Of course, she'd checked him for wounds after the rogue fight, but she hadn't been that thorough. Even a tiny scratch could be enough to turn a human.

Or kill him.

As if on cue, a shadow flickered in the front windows, and there was Cole.

Mate! Her wolf practically jumped to attention and wagged its tail. Plopped its butt on the ground and arranged its front paws just so, so that if he turned his head and used X-ray vision, he'd see a perfectly friendly, tame wolf.

And he did turn his head. Stopped dead in his tracks and peered in the windows as if he'd sensed her there.

"Hi, Cole!" Jessica waved cheerily.

He waved back and flashed his perfect smile.

Mate! her wolf cried. *Mate!*

She rushed out onto the sidewalk then screeched to a halt in front of him, panting. Searching his eyes for the telltale sparks of a Changeling.

"Heya, Janna."

"Hi, Cole," she mumbled, running her hands up his arms. She hung on tight in relief, because his eyes were normal. Well, normal for Cole, which meant dark and stormy, with shafts of silverish sunlight cutting through the clouds. But no stray sparks, no fireworks, thank God.

She reeled him into a huge hug of relief and laughed into his ear.

"What?" He looked at her with a grin.

She shook her head. "Just happy to see you." *Happy to see you human. Happy to see you okay.*

Which had its own set of issues, she realized as she led him through the café for a muffin, then into the saloon. He was human. She was shifter. Getting involved with Cole could draw the wrath of the Blue Bloods.

You will pay with your lives...

She hid her shiver in a bouncy step and led him over to his favorite spot at the bar.

Getting involved with Cole meant putting her sister and the bear brothers at risk, and they were all the family she had.

Them, and Cole, too, her wolf chipped in.

She took a deep breath and forced herself to let go of his arm.

"So, what can I get you?"

"Coffee, please." His eyebrow curved when he asked, and she melted all over again.

"More coffee here, too," the guys in the corner called. "Simon, can you turn on the TV?"

She hurried off for the pot of coffee then zipped back to Cole, placed a mug before him, and poured. Just watching him smile made her go warm all over again.

He leaned over to whisper in her ear. "Love your coffee."

Love! Her wolf grabbed the word like a bone and paraded around with it. *He loves me! Loves me!*

She wanted to smack the beast and yell, *Coffee, dummy. He loves the coffee.* But the way his eyes locked on hers made it easy to believe he meant something else.

She smiled shyly, and he smiled back. Touched her arm and sent crazy messages zipping around her body.

Then the television blared to life behind them, and Cole froze.

"A beautiful day here in Las Vegas for the annual bull-riding championships!" the announcer beamed.

Cole didn't swivel his stool to watch or turn his head. Didn't make the slightest motion. He sat stiff as a statue as the show went on.

"We've got a great day for you," a second announcer chipped in and started going over the program for the day.

"Janna, can we get refills?" one of the ranch hands asked.

She dragged herself away from Cole and filled each of their mugs while peeking at the screen. Furious bulls twisted, turned, and tore up the arena. The men riding them jolted and jerked like puppets. Janna winced as one man after another crashed to the ground, then scrambled out of the way of charging bulls. Crowds cheered, buzzers buzzed, and the announcer went through a high-speed introduction of the competitors and the bulls. There was one named Gruesome, another named Haunted Hollow, and a third called Dante's Inferno.

Janna glanced at Cole, whose face was a mask.

One of the Twin Moon ranch hands seated in the corner pointed as the television replayed a cowboy flying off a raging bull in slow motion.

"Just like you flying off that bull at the ranch, Jake."

Jake flashed a good-natured smile and pulled up his sleeve. "I still have the bruise. Check it out."

"Yeah, and a matching one on your ass," his friend taunted, then remembered Janna was there. "Sorry, sweetheart."

She barely noticed, still staring at Jake's arm. She'd rarely seen a bruise on a shifter simply because they healed so quickly. Which meant Jake must have taken a hell of a fall.

"This new Brangus-Criollo hybrid we're trying out sure don't like to be ridden."

"Don't like much of anything," another one griped.

Janna looked over at Cole, who had clamped down so hard on the brass rail of the bar, his knuckles were white.

"Uh, guys, can you watch this somewhere else?" she tried.

"Are you kidding?" one protested. "It's the finals, Janna. The finals!"

She nodded. Bull-riding finals that Cole really, really didn't want to see or even hear. Why, she didn't know. Only that he looked stonier than ever before.

"So that's the lineup for today, along with the top bull-fighters in the country to keep the riders safe." The camera switched back to the announcer, who turned to his co-commentator. "Sonny, how do you think last year's tragedy will affect the riders here today?"

She halted in midstep and stared at the screen, where the man called Sonny was sadly shaking his head. Tragedy?

"Well, Frank, they're pros. I know they've all thought about it, but they've got to come into the arena with clear heads today."

"A terrible, terrible thing," the announcer agreed, and the saloon went quiet but for the faint squeak of the ceiling fans. "Now, folks, some of you might want not want to watch this. Out of respect to the bull rider and his family, we won't show the worst, but we feel it's important to highlight the heroics of our pro bullfighting team."

She watched, slack-jawed, as the view switched to another bull charging out of a pen marked with last year's date. A replay of the event they were talking about.

"It started like any other ride..."

The sound switched to the voice of a different announcer. "And now we have Hammersmith, coming out of the pen..."

37

A huge black bull tore into the arena, bucking wildly.

"And at this point, A.J. looked to be in control..." the live commentator said over the voice of the replay.

The bull bowed its head, then snapped it up, bringing its horns within inches of the rider's face.

"But watch when Hammersmith goes into his next spin..."

Janna didn't want to watch, but she couldn't *not* watch as the sound changed, going from the present-day announcers to the voice that had commented on the scene live.

"He's down! He's down!" the live announcer screamed.

Janna watched in horror as the young rider flew off the bull and crashed headfirst at an unnatural angle in the middle of the arena. The image cut away just before impact, but it didn't take much imagination to fill in the blanks.

"Shit," one of the ranch hands muttered under his breath.

"Doctors reckon the vertebrae were broken right there," the original commentator said over the voice of the other. "Nothing no helmet's gonna do about that."

A horrified gasp rang out from the audience, followed by shouts as the bull wheeled to charge the limp body.

"Look at our bullfighters move in!" the live commentator shouted. "Look at that! Look at that!"

The coffee mug shook in Janna's hand shook as she watched three men dart forward.

"This is why we don't call them rodeo clowns, folks..." the commentator said of the three men.

"Watch the one in blue..."

Out of the corner of her eye, she saw Cole go stiff. But her focus remained on the screen, where the fastest of the three bullfighters darted between the bull and the limp body in the dirt, trying to distract it. He sprinted right into the bull's field of vision, but the bull was intent on the fallen rider.

Any normal human would duck out of the way, but the bullfighter in blue planted himself right in the bull's way, daring the animal to attack him.

"Seventeen hundred pounds of charging bull, folks, and this man's holding his ground." The announcer whistled.

The bull lowered its horns and thundered on.

"Get out of the way, man," one of the ranch hands murmured at the screen.

The other two bullfighters waved and hollered from each side, trying to draw away the bull — to no avail.

Janna shook her head at the impossibility of it all. If the bullfighter moved, the charging beast would trample the fallen rider. But if the bullfighter stayed, *he'd* get trampled.

She watched, frozen, as the man put his hands out and grabbed the bull's horns. The animal snapped his head upward, lifting the man.

"Look at that!" the announcer screamed as the man threw his weight to the side.

"Jesus, that guy has balls," another ranch hand muttered.

The bull's head twisted to the side, all his fury focused on his new foe. It cleared the injured man by an inch and bulldozed onward, trying to trample the bullfighter. The man dragged his feet, trying to stay clear of the hooves. Somehow, he found enough traction to spring to one side and then ducked as the bull jabbed his horns right. Dashed to the left again...

"That's what you call a pro, folks," the announcer murmured.

It went on like that for another minute, with an unrelenting bullfighter and an equally determined bull, until finally a man on a horse charged in and drove the bull away.

Cole slid off his seat and headed for the saloon doors without saying a word, but Janna's eyes stayed rooted on the TV. There was something about the bullfighter on the screen...

She watched the man in blue rush to the injured man's side as medics sprinted across the arena with a stretcher. He crouched over the fallen bull rider, then backed away to give the medical team space.

"God, it doesn't look good," the event announcer said in a hush.

The bullfighter backed up for a good ten feet before turning toward the camera. After two more steps, he collapsed to one knee. He spent a long time there before the other two bullfighters came along, slapped him on the back, and pulled him to his feet.

A tall man with sandy hair.

Holy shit.

Cole. That was Cole, being pulled to his feet.

The television switched back to this year's announcer, who shook his head sadly. "Real heroes, those bullfighters. The doctors did what they could, but a broken neck is a broken neck..."

She shut her eyes.

"Scenes that will haunt all of us..." the announcer said.

She turned to the saloon doors, which were still flapping from Cole's silent exit. She shook her head. Cole...

A second later, she darted outside, following him.

Chapter Five

Cole strode down the sidewalk, barely aware of the space in front of him. His ears rang, and his nose tickled with the scent of angry bull. Instead of the street, all he saw was the arena. All in his memory, but all so clear.

He's down! He's down! the announcer had screamed.

He winced at the memory of the fallen rider, lying in the dirt. Not getting up. Never getting up again.

God, if only he hadn't talked to the kid earlier that day. The rider, A.J., was a rookie on the bull-riding scene. Cocky on the outside, nervous as hell on the inside because he'd drawn the rankest bull in the lineup. Cole knew; he'd seen the kid an hour before his ride, hunched over the bathroom sink, staring at nothing.

"You got this, kid." He'd opened his big mouth, slapped the kid on the back, and shot him a you-can-do-this smile.

Jesus, he'd sent the guy to his death.

The kid forced a stiff nod and echoed his words. "I got this."

When the kid's turn came up, Cole could see the same nervous twitch in his eye. The kind of anxiety a rider couldn't afford to carry into the arena.

One of the handlers at the chute gave the kid a reassuring look that said, *Nothing wrong with pulling out.* But the crowd was cheering, the bull snorting — everything was ready for the rider's eight seconds of fame.

And for whatever reason, the kid looked to Cole. Right at him with eyes that begged, *What the hell do I do?*

Cole gave the kid a thumbs-up that said, *You got this.*

He might as well have filled in a death certificate, because the guy had nodded, mounted up, and seconds later...

He watched the bull twist and throw the rider. Heard the crack as the kid landed on his neck. The guy was still alive when Cole got to him, after the bull had finally been driven away. Still wheezing, still wide-eyed with panic. Still totally limp.

"You'll be okay," Cole had lied. Twice. Then he'd backed away and let the medics in, because they could make a miracle happen, right?

He shook his head as he stomped down the sidewalk. No miracle. No happy end. And the worst part was everyone insisting on patting him on the back as if he'd truly helped.

No, the worst was the letter he'd gotten from the kid's mother a few weeks later. A goddamn thank-you letter he'd burned the first chance he got, though the words were permanently seared into his memory.

Thank you for doing everything you could to help my son...
Christ. If only she knew.

He fumbled with the key to his truck and glared at his own haggard reflection in the window. Some fucking hero. Some fucking help.

Footsteps rushed up behind him, but he reached for the door handle without turning.

"Cole."

For the first time in weeks, hearing Janna's voice didn't turn everything inside him to mush.

"Cole!"

He stayed still, gripping the door handle so hard, his knuckles turned white.

When she patted him on the back, part of him wanted to give in to her soft touch. To turn and hug her and let her be the one to whisper in his ear. But he couldn't. Wouldn't. Shouldn't.

"You gonna be okay?" she asked. Softly, like he might break.

"Sure," he said through tight lips. And he was. It was A.J. who wasn't okay.

"I mean..."

"Fine," he barked, scratching madly at his arm.

Janna's eyes followed the gesture, and her brow furrowed. "Are you hurt?"

He shook his head. His arm didn't really hurt. Scratching the itch had become a habit, that was all.

"Cole..." She turned him around, locked her eyes on his, and for a second, he was submerged in the deep blue. But then she gasped slightly, and her eyes went wide. "What's wrong?"

Other than the fact that he'd ushered an innocent man to his death?

"Did you get hurt in the fight? I mean, the fight in the saloon that night?"

It took his mind a second to jump from bull riding to the night she and Jessica were held up by those thugs. The night he'd helped Janna out of a pickle and ended up thrown into a wall.

"Been thrown worse than that."

"I mean, cut."

"No," he said, rubbing his arm, then hiding the motion.

Too late. Janna pulled his arm toward her and tugged his sleeve up.

"It's nothing, Janna." He pulled back but stopped when she gasped at the pink swelling.

"No..."

Kind of overreacting over a tiny scratch, wasn't she?

Her gaze snapped back to his eyes, studying him as if for some sign.

"It's fine," he insisted.

"Did this happen that night?"

"It's fine. Been a little slow to heal, that's all."

Even as he said it, it sounded like a lie.

Not just a scratch, a raspy inner voice warned. *Never going to heal...*

He yanked the truck door open.

Need her. Need our mate, the voice said, more insistently every time, until it wasn't telling or asking but demanding and flooding him with dark images again. Of grabbing Janna and exposing her neck. Baring his jaws wide and biting right into her flesh...

Mine! Mate!

He shook the horrifying image away and closed the door between them, trying to keep her safe. That voice was evil. He had to keep Janna away from it. Which meant keeping her away from him, for her own sake.

"Gotta go," he mumbled, pushing the key into the ignition.

"Wait, Cole!" Her voice was so sharp, so uncompromising, that he obeyed. She pulled the red bandana from her neck and tied it around his. "Here. Take this."

"But..." He didn't promise, but he couldn't bring himself to snatch it off, either.

He shook his head, more at himself and the voice inside that was also yelling, *But! But!* There was no but. Another minute listening to that voice and he'd throw Janna into the back of the truck and make off with her. Take her somewhere quiet and do who knows what to her.

"A little reminder of me." Her worried smile was forced.

"Gotta go," he murmured and fired up the truck.

He didn't want to go, but he sure as hell couldn't stay. So he drove. Somewhere. Anywhere. Staring straight ahead to avoid the image of a forlorn Janna in the side mirror, and his own reflection in the rearview. He took the first left he could to break the contact and only released his white-knuckled grip on the wheel to punch the dashboard. He drove too fast, then too slow, utterly without direction or a sense of time. He ducked his head to scan every part of the daytime sky for a hint of the moon. Although it was nowhere in sight, he could feel it lurking out there, ready to leap out and toy with him again. The very thought made his skin tickle, his nerves crawl.

On instinct, he tugged Janna's bandana up to his nose and inhaled. Her scent settled him, a teensy tiny bit. He sniffed it like a drug and drove a little more. A lot more, actually, on a loop of the whole damn county until he found himself pulling into his parking space at Rosalind's place. He stalked toward the barn, ignoring the dog scrambling away and the horses pawing the ground.

Rosalind was across the way, showing a couple of newcomers around. A vacationing family come to stay at the little studio apartment Ros rented out, judging by the clothes, the camera, and the heap of luggage. There was a dad, a mom, and two squirming little kids. Normally, he'd go over and introduce himself, but hell, in the state he was in, he'd probably scare them away.

He stomped to the work shed, grabbed a hammer and a can of nails, and set out to mend the broken paddock on the far side of the property — the far, far side. Banging at metal with metal suited his mood right now just fine. But even the din he made didn't squelch the voices in his head.

Must have my mate! Must, or I'll die!

He shook his head hard enough to rattle the voice away. Wondered if it was true. Wondered how much he'd mind dying. Maybe that was the best way out. He looked up and across the valley to where the abandoned train tracks lay. It didn't take much to imagine an old-time locomotive rushing along, blowing a trail of steam. He imagined balancing on his toes on the tracks and watching it sweep closer, head on. The whistle would scream, the rails would vibrate, and it would be right on top of him, until, *bam!* The end.

A fly buzzed past his ear, and he went back to hammering. Wishing. Wondering.

Chapter Six

Janna shook all the way back to the saloon, and when she grabbed for the coffeepot to make another round of the customers, she made such a clatter, everyone in the saloon looked up.

"Sorry," she mumbled, trying desperately not to turn around and chase Cole down for a second time.

Mate! Must help our mate! her wolf shrieked, clawing wildly at the door of the mental cage she kept it locked behind.

She ground her teeth and took a deep breath. Cole needed some time, and holy cow, she did, too. She'd caught a glimpse of his eyes before he hurried away, and the gray-on-gray storm clouds she loved gazing at had bolts of lightning in them now. The classic sign of a Changeling, or so she'd heard.

Cole. Changeling. Wolf?

Mine! Mate!

She closed her eyes, trying to process it all. It wasn't withdrawal that had made Cole moody these past few weeks — it was the Change happening inside him. Slowly perhaps, due to the small size of the scratch, but inexorably. And now, the transformation was accelerating.

No wonder her wolf had suddenly gone bonkers for him. As long as Cole was fully human, fate could keep her mate disguised. But now that he was turning into a shifter, his scent had intensified. Magnified. Maximized, so there was no mistaking it.

He was the one! Hers! Her destined mate!

Her heart pounded in her chest, so fast and hard, it felt like her ribcage might crack. She grabbed at the edge of the counter, fighting the overwhelmingly giddy feeling of it all.

47

Jesus, it really did happen. Destiny, bringing two souls together. Forever.

Her heart skipped, but her stomach lurched, remembering the way Cole stood beside his pickup. She'd cringed when she saw what he'd unconsciously done as she approached — namely, testing the air with his nose. Swinging his head left and right like a wolf following a faint trail. Tipping his chin up.

When his eyes met hers, the storm gray was lit with tiny flashes of green and brown. A telltale indicator of a Changeling — or man going slowly mad.

She wanted to grab him by the hand, race to her car, and drive far, far away.

As if that would work. As if she could outrun fate.

Her wolf raised its nose and let out a long, mournful howl.

Humans wounded by shifters usually died a drawn-out and painful death. Only a tiny minority survived, and most of those went slowly mad. Only the tiniest fraction survived — like Kyle Williams, the Twin Moon wolf who worked as a state cop. He and Rick Rivera, Tina Hawthorne's mate, were the only two survivors Janna knew of. Women bitten by male shifters had a much higher survival rate because their bodies didn't fight the Change the same way. But men... The stronger the man, the more his body would resist the Change. The more he'd struggle to his own death.

And Cole... Her eyes slid to the rodeo still running on the TV. Jesus, if ever a man was a candidate for driving himself mad, it was Cole. A man already carrying way too many ghosts and too much guilt.

"Hi, Janna," a voice called from the door.

Her chin snapped up as she forced a smile on her face.

Stef, a lean, lanky she-wolf from Twin Moon pack, stood at the door with her mate, Kyle.

Janna stared for a moment, because Stef had once been all-human herself, just like her mate, Kyle — another human who had survived the Change. They ambled in like it was just another sunny day in northern Arizona, swinging a baby carrier in which a tiny little bundle slept.

48

Janna grabbed her drinks tray and hurried over to the side booth they took, trying to exude a calm she didn't feel. Shifters could see — and more importantly, smell — right through each other's guises, so she had to cloak her feelings well.

"Can I get you the lunch menu?" she asked, studying Kyle out of the corner of her eye.

Plenty of women did that on account of the way the man looked. *Fine, mighty fine,* she'd heard more than one woman sigh whenever the cop shifter stopped by the saloon. He came by often, on and off duty as a state cop, and always on duty as a leading member of Twin Moon pack — the pack that leased the saloon to the Voss brothers and wanted to make damn sure it didn't become a magnet for shifters of the wrong type.

Kyle's eyes were firmly on Stef's. His hand clasped hers tightly, and the love pulsing between the two of them might as well have been a glowing neon light.

"Just a piece of pie for me." Stef smiled.

"And you?" Janna asked, sneaking a peek at the open collar of Kyle's shirt, where the red edge of one of his scars barely showed.

As a human, Kyle had been mauled by a rogue shifter. That was years ago, but Janna had heard the stories of how hard his body had fought the Change and how close he'd tiptoed to death. But Kyle had had his happy ending. He'd found his place in the pack, met his destined mate, and settled down with her in every sense of the word.

If he could do it, so could Cole, right?

She held her breath, hoping for some voice to rise out of the desert and whisper an affirmative response.

Kyle had come that close to death because his wounds had been so severe and the Change came over him suddenly, unlike Cole's slower transformation, right?

Right? she wanted to scream, cueing the answer she craved. *Right?*

She strained her ears but didn't hear a peep.

"Just coffee for me," Kyle said.

"Nothing for baby?" she managed a feeble joke.

The two shifters turned to the baby carrier with the happy grins of proud parents and peered in at their sleeping little boy.

"I think he's good," Stef said.

He's perfect, Kyle's proud daddy eyes said.

Janna heaved a huge inner sigh and turned for the kitchen. Kyle was living proof that a man could survive the Change. And Tina's mate Rick had survived it, too. Two perfectly good examples of why she needn't fear for Cole.

She racked her mind for more and came up painfully blank. All she came up with were a dozen ugly examples to the contrary. So, Jesus, what should she do?

She glanced through the serving window from the kitchen to the saloon. Theoretically, she ought to inform the wolves who owned the saloon and oversaw this area of the Southwest when it came to shifter matters. But the Twin Moon alpha, Ty Hawthorne, could be a downright terrifying man to confront.

Janna considered approaching Ty's sister Tina but discarded it almost as quickly. Tina had a soft spot for wayward shifters, but the saloon had already brought trouble too close to Twin Moon pack, and her patience had to be nearing an end. And with a human mate of her own, Tina had to be just as wary of the Blue Bloods as Janna.

No, she couldn't tell anyone. Not yet.

Mate! Needs us! her wolf whined inside.

The pull toward him was like a physical thing, a stretch of every nerve in her body. Another hour without him and she'd go nuts.

She slumped as soon as the word crossed her mind. Going nuts. That fate awaited Cole if she didn't do anything to help. But what? There were no recipes for seeing a Changeling through the transformation. Nothing but hope and faith — two things she'd been awfully short of ever since fleeing Montana.

That thought tipped her from desperation over to anger. She'd done enough running, not enough fighting. And she'd had enough.

Enough! her wolf agreed, baring its teeth. *No more running!*

She had to get to Cole. Had to talk to him and try to explain. The full moon was only a few nights away, so she had to do something fast.

But she couldn't exactly run off after Cole at the beginning of her shift, and it would kill her to wait. That problem had to be solved first.

She delivered the pie and coffee to Kyle and Stef, then hustled to the café door and yanked off her apron.

"Jess!" she called into the café next door. "Can you cover for me for a while?"

Jess made an unhappy noise. "I've got so much to do..."

"Kyle and Stef are here with their baby. Their cute, adorable—"

Jess came speeding out the door and into the saloon, grinning ear to ear. "Baby? Why didn't you tell me?"

Janna trotted off for her car, shaking her head. Problem one was solved. Problem two...

She steeled her shoulders and picked up her pace.

Chapter Seven

Cole spent a sweaty hour repairing the fence, alternating between hammering and sniffing from Janna's bandana. That and the clean scent of pine that started where the property merged with the forest made him feel a little more sane.

Rosalind put the guests' kids on a pony and led them around the ring while the parents snapped pictures, but he kept his distance, just in case. Kept his head and eyes down, too, so they'd know to leave him alone.

But then a truck pulled into the paddocks adjoining Rosalind's place and slowly backed up to the gate. When human voices mixed with animal bellows drifted to his ears, he couldn't help but look up.

The trailer the truck had hauled in rattled and shook with the sharp bang of hooves. Something very big and very ornery wanted out of that trailer, bad.

"Moo!" One of the little kids, fresh off his pony ride, ran over to the fence. The sound of his voice carried. "Moo!"

"Big moo," the dad said, watching three men tilt the trailer's ramp down.

Cole's ears twitched. Could he really hear their voices from so far away?

"Hmmf." That was Rosalind, who rented the spare paddocks to stock traders on occasion. She sure didn't look happy at what they had unloaded this time.

"Hey! Hey!" One of the handlers whistled and yelled, and the spotted rump of a huge bull appeared.

It bellowed, twisted, and banged away, taking one step forward for every two back. One of those ornery Longhorn-Brahman mixes that liked to fight every inch of the way. The inexperienced handlers were making things worse, too, riling the beast up more than settling it down.

Cole shook his head, watching the men force the beast down the ramp with a whip and a prod. No wonder the bull was so pissed off.

With a snort, the animal clomped down the ramp and trotted across the paddock, bucking and kicking at an invisible foe.

Cole squinted into the sun to watch it in spite of himself. He studied how the bull dipped its shoulders before lifting its hips, and how it twisted to the right. Getting a feel for the animal's patterns out of sheer habit.

The bull was huge. Angry. Wild. A product of overly aggressive breeding practices was Cole's guess, because big money called for ever bigger, meaner, wilder bulls to challenge riders. Breeders were succeeding, too, because the percentage of riders completing eight-second rides had dropped dramatically in recent years. Some bulls were downright unrideable, and it wouldn't surprise Cole if this was one of those.

"Bad bull," Rosalind told the little boy in the red T-shirt and brown overalls. "You stay away."

Cole contemplated the fencepost in front of him for a long time. He'd stayed away, all right. Practically run away from anything to do with cattle, even though it was in his blood. He'd grown up on a ranch, got his start bullfighting on a ranch, spent his whole life doing what he loved best, until...

Yeah, until last year.

He glanced up at the bull huffing and puffing at the far corner of the enclosure and imagined those wide, red-ringed eyes up close.

It wasn't bulls that scared him. It was fate, swooping down out of nowhere to grab one life and send the soul of another spiraling into an abyss.

Everyone said it was best to get back in the saddle after a fall, but he hadn't gotten around to that. He doubted he ever would, because what if something he did led to another meaningless death?

Something on the breeze mocked him. *Maybe you are just scared.*

He grimaced and went back to hammering. Missing twice for every hit, cursing every time.

The dust trail of an approaching vehicle came down the drive, and he wondered who was coming now.

Mine! Mate!

He jumped to his feet as he recognized the battered little Mitsubishi Janna was so proud of.

Janna! Janna! his soul sang as she pulled in.

Part of him wanted to run straight to her and pull her into his arms; the other wanted to run for the hills. What if that inner voice got out of control again? What if he went too far and hurt her one day?

Would never hurt my mate, the voice growled back.

She got out of the car and looked around briefly before turning exactly in his direction. It was as if she'd sensed him the way he'd sensed her coming down the drive. She was a good quarter mile away, but even so, that feeling of standing barefoot in a mountain meadow trickled slowly into his soul.

She'd come to see him! His heart thumped inside his chest. She wanted him. Maybe even needed him the way he needed her.

Rosalind had once boarded a fancy Arabian mare with a long, glossy mane for a week, and the way it pranced around the paddock put all the other horses to shame. That's what Janna looked like, gliding across the way. Never mind the dust, the beat-up cars, and peeling paint of the barn: she rose above it all, shining like a jewel amidst pebbles. Making the whole place classier just by being in it, the way she did at the saloon. But she fit in at the same time, like a princess who'd been mixed up with a cowgirl at birth and had grown up working a ranch.

He entertained himself with silly notions like that as she started up his way. It was a good, long way, and that was fine with him, because he could relish the moment longer, watching her smile, her springy step, her easy, flowing gait.

Heya, Janna, he'd say when she got closer and try to play it cool.

Heya, Cole, she'd answer and maybe even tilt her chin up for a kiss.

But neither one of them got around to saying anything, because when Janna was still a couple of hundred yards away, another voice screeched.

"Johnny! No!"

Both of them spun toward the stock pens, where someone was running. Pointing. Yelling.

"Stop! Oh my God, stop!"

A second person was climbing the split-rail fence and yelling, too. "Johnny! Johnny!"

It took him precious seconds to zoom in on the spot they gestured toward. A little blur of red in the dirt of the pens. A little kid.

"Johnny!" a woman screamed, but the kid just ran on. More voices joined the first two, and a dog started to bark.

"Moo!" the kid cried in glee. Just a little guy in overalls, having a great time outfoxing his parents, who clung to the fence and waved at him madly as he ran on. "Moo!"

The bull in the far corner of the paddock perked up its ears. Its nostrils flared. One massive hoof pawed the ground, and its white-rimmed eyes narrowed on the child.

Oh, shit.

"Stop!" another voice called. It was Janna, streaking into the paddock when no one else dared to, chasing down the kid. She had her hair in a ponytail, and it whipped behind her as she ran full tilt.

"Jesus," he muttered, running for the fence from where he'd been on the hill. He scrambled over the three rungs, swung himself over the top rail, and leaped into the corral. "Janna!"

Janna didn't stop, though. Not even when the bull snorted and swung its head and massive horns her way.

Cole hit the ground, sprinting hard. Trying to intercept Janna and the kid and bull, all at the same time. His feet pounded the ground, but it seemed to take forever, because that was his woman out there.

The bull roared and barreled straight at the boy, who froze and gaped like a deer in the middle of a highway. A deer about to get plowed down by an eighteen-wheeler in the ugliest possible way.

Voices sounded from all sides, but all Cole saw was the scene ahead. He saw the bull, eating up the distance to its target. Saw Janna, closing in on the kid. She scooped the child up without slowing her fleet feet and raced straight for the fence on the other side.

The bull leaned left, altering course to intercept her.

"Oh my God! Oh my God!" a not-too-helpful onlooker screamed.

Cole kicked into another gear, too busy running to utter a sound. If he had a spare breath, he'd use it to blurt a string of curses that would reach over the state line.

Pip the dog ran in and raced right for the bull, who lowered his head and swiped sideways, missing the mutt by an inch. The bull barely broke its step, though. It was still locked on to Janna and the kid wailing in her arms.

"Faster!" someone shouted, as if Janna hadn't thought of that.

"Janna!" he yelled. Two damn syllables when his mind was crowded with a whole string of instructions he could never get out in time. *Cut back my way. Over here to your right. Head off at an angle and run for your life.*

But her name was all he could get out. No time for anything more than that and a frantic prayer. "Janna!"

She ran on, then made an abrupt cut right — precisely the way he'd envisioned. His heart skipped a beat, then pounded on. He was closer now, but the bull was closer, too.

He yanked the bandana off his neck and wrapped one end around his fist. Snapped it in the air while running full tilt and hissing at the bull.

Over here, motherfucker. Over here.

Janna sprinted on, following the exact path he would have marked in the dirt for her if he'd have had the time. As if they'd mapped it all out ahead of time on a chalkboard or a secret playbook.

Inwardly, he cheered Janna on. Outwardly, he went on hissing and snapping the bandana at the bull.

Two dark eyes and the points of two very sharp horns swung his way, and the bull snorted. It might as well have rubbed its hooves together and chuckled, *Now, now. What's this?*

Cole pulled up in his tracks and looked the bull square in the eye, challenging it.

This is where you need to attack. He whistled in a way even the stupidest bull would understand. *Come and get me.*

The bull snorted, lowered its horns, and charged.

Elation briefly coursed through his veins, and he nearly pumped his fist. He'd gotten the beast away from Janna and the child!

The icy truth belted him a second later. Two thousand pounds of angry bull was heading straight his way, and it was going for the kill.

It was exactly the situation he'd willingly put himself in thousands of times, back when he was still doing the job he loved. The rush, the edge, the split-second timing. The battle of wits, of man versus beast. He could saddle up tired trail horses in his sleep. But this kind of all-or-nothing duel...

Nothing came close. Nothing.

He balanced on the balls of his feet, waved the bandana as far from his body as he could, and counted down the inches between him and the colossus. If he had his fellow bullfighters to help out, this wouldn't be half as suicidal. Teasing a bull wasn't as crazy as people imagined if you worked with a good team. And he and Frank and George had been the best. Forming a triangle, taking turns drawing the bull away from the man closest to its horns. Knowing just when to jump in and when to dart the hell away.

A team gave you the edge you needed. A team gave you a chance.

Which meant he was screwed. Well and truly screwed. He was alone. A single target for a single, raging bull. No triangle. No padding, no armored vest. And no backup, except for Rosalind's hysterical mutt, yipping madly at the bull's heels.

The bull thundered up, and Cole reached out as if to catch it. He wheeled at the last second, missing the horns by a hair.

Darting left before the bull could bulldoze under him, he got clear while the animal's momentum carried it away.

A breather. He had a half-second breather in which to figure some way out of a mess no sane bullfighter would ever find himself in — namely, in the middle of an open paddock, with what seemed like miles to the nearest fence he might leap over. No chute to trick the bull into, no mounted backup. No one there to count on but himself. He glanced left and spotted Janna, closing in on the fence and safety. Thank God for that.

The bull bellowed and came around for a second charge. A bull who didn't like losing, from the looks of it.

Cole kept his left shoulder to it and sidestepped away. Slowly, because it wasn't about outrunning the bull. Just about timing. Perfect timing. He didn't bother with the bandana this time, because the bull would see past that trick.

"Right here, mister." He could see the whites of the bull's eyes, the pink flare of its nostrils. "Right here."

The ground rumbled as the bull closed in. Cole gathered his weight on his right foot and stretched out his arms. Warding off a bull as heavy as that would never work, but it would give him a sense of the animal's momentum and help him adjust.

The bull grunted and lowered its horns. Sneaky bastard, going for Cole's feet. It practically plowed a line through the dirt, kicking up dust as it chose exactly the right moment to pop up.

Cole was faster by a hair. He spun away fast enough to miss being gored, but not fast enough to miss altogether. The bull smacked his ass with the flat of its forehead and lifted him clear off his feet.

Airtime. Cole splayed his arms, trying to control his flight. He felt suspended in space and time, watching it tick slowly by. He kept his feet under him because landing this wrong would make him dead meat.

Jesus. This wasn't just airtime, but *major* airtime, giving him plenty of time to think. About life, about death. About the bull waiting to finish him off.

The ground grew closer... closer...

The air left his lungs as he hit the dirt running. Snorting like a bull, because the air was full of dust churned up by four massive feet.

He cut out of the way just as the bull came charging again, and this time, the bull turned on a dime. Jabbed its horns, curved past, then raised its hips...

Cole saw the bottom of the beast's curved hooves, aimed for his skull. The air whooshed over his head as he ducked instinctively. Ducked his whole body, turtling his head in, because the hooves were sweeping right over him now. Fifteen hundred pounds of beast swept an inch above him in a merciless kick aimed to shoot Cole right off the planet and into outer space.

Whoosh!

Cole backpedaled just in time to see the bull's hoof slice the air in front of his face.

Holy shit. The bull had missed by a hair. The thinnest hair ever.

Woof woof woof woof woof! Pip barked hysterically, buying him time to get away. If he survived this day, he'd get that dog the biggest damn bone any canine had ever seen.

A whip cracked in the air, and Cole flinched as if another opponent had appeared, ready to flay his hide. A glance up showed Rosalind, high on the top rail of the fence, cracking her old leather whip at the bull like a geriatric version of Indiana Jones.

"Hey! Hey!" she hollered at the top of her lungs.

Cole ran for the fence in the millisecond that the bull paused. He didn't dare look back, just sprinted for his life, the way Janna and Rosalind screamed for him to do. The ground behind him shook like there was a whole herd of bison hot on his heels. A tiny whoosh sounded — the lift of the bull's horns, aimed at his back.

He leaped for the fence with every muscle in his body. Stretching his arms, straining forward an inch ahead of those horns.

And *bang!* He smashed into the top rail just as Rosalind cracked the whip, making the bull wheel away an inch before it barreled into the fence.

"Jesus, Cole." Janna's eyes were huge.

A couple of strong hands grabbed his shirt and hauled him over to the sane side of the fence, and people started smacking him on the back. Some of those smacks were of the *what-the-hell-were-you-thinking* type, while others said, *Good job.*

"Damn good job," Rosalind murmured as he coughed and hacked and sneezed, hunched over with his hands on his knees. Not quite shaking inside, but close.

"Oh my God, oh my God..." The mother all but crushed the boy to her chest while Janna calmed her down.

"It's all good. It's all right."

Cole drank in the sight of that mother, holding her son. Rocking him. Crying in nerve-rattling fear but smiling at the same time. And when she looked up with gratitude pouring from her eyes — the most sincere kind of gratitude that never quite made it to the tongue — Cole held his breath.

That gratitude was aimed at him.

You saved him, Janna's look said. *You saved a future. You did that, Cole.*

Her proud gaze stayed on him, determined to knock the message into his thick head.

"Thank you. Thank you so much," the father said again and again.

Thank you. Words a man heard a thousand times in his life, but not always that waterlogged with emotion, and not always for all the right reasons. But today...

Cole tilted his head back, looked at the sky, and gulped a couple of times. He replayed it all in his mind but got stuck on one part over and over again. The image of the bull, heading straight for Janna.

He grabbed her hand and pulled her away from the hysterical voices, away from the pacing bull still looking for a way through the fence. Over to the shade of the barn, where he ran his hands over her shoulders again and again.

"Are you okay?" He said it a thousand times, not quite ready to let the fear for her go.

"I'm fine. Cole, I'm fine."

Didn't seem to matter how often she said that, though. He needed to be sure. He smoothed her hair, touched her face. Held her smaller, softer hands in his and checked them, too, until he buried her in a hug he wasn't about to let her out of anytime soon.

"I'm okay, Cole. You're the one who was nearly gored."

He shook his head. Didn't she know how little his life mattered and how much hers did?

"You could have been killed," he murmured.

"Believe me, I'm hard to kill." When she laughed and pulled back, her eyes sparkled with some private joke. But then again, Janna's eyes always sparkled. She ran a hand over his cheek before submitting to another full-body crush.

"I'm fine, Cole."

Her voice was muffled. Her hands slid around his waist, and finally, finally, his heart slowed down a little bit. Fear gradually slipped back and gave way to warmer, calmer things. Like how nice her hair smelled. How good it was to feel her heart beating against his. How perfectly her body fit against his. Not too small, not too big. Just right.

So right that, before he knew it, he was touching her again, and in a whole different way. Nuzzling her ear. Sliding his hands over her body, tracing her perfect curves instead of checking for broken bones.

She tilted her head up, and the second their lips met, he knew that was only the start.

Her fingers tightened on his shirt, and her eyes had that feral shine they got sometimes.

"Cole," she whispered in a husky voice.

The scent of arousal filled the space around them, and for once, he didn't wonder how the hell he knew what that was.

"Janna." He held her hand tighter and tugged her up the stairs.

Chapter Eight

Janna wrestled with her inner wolf as they started up the stairs.

We came to talk to him, not screw him!

But her protests were halfhearted, and her wolf knew it.

Not waiting a second longer to bond with my mate! the beast growled back.

Bond. Screw. Fuck. Whichever term she used, the danger was still there. Sleeping with Cole would bring his wolf closer to the surface — a dangerous proposition. But doing so would also bring their souls closer, which might help save him when the transformation began.

Exactly, her wolf agreed quickly. *And besides. . .*

Janna tightened her grip on Cole's shirt, knowing just what the *besides* was. She was hungry for her mate. Starving. Craving him in a way she'd never craved any man.

"Janna," he whispered in her ear.

The little control she had left went into making sure her nails didn't turn into claws and rip off his shirt. Just seeing him at work on the fence from across the property had set her off. There was a brooding kind of animal energy coming off him. And watching him confront the bull tipped her right over the edge.

A good mate! A brave one, who protects what is his! Her wolf nodded eagerly.

If she were in a clearer frame of mind, she might have shrugged the thought away, because she didn't need anyone's protection. She could take care of herself.

Except, of course, Cole had rescued her twice now.

Time for us to rescue him.

She let her tongue tangle with his and her limbs give in to his insistent pull. Tasting the animal in him for the first time made her inch a little closer to the end of her wolf's leash. The voice she'd strained to hear back in the saloon was shouting in her ear, banishing her last doubts.

This man is your mate. Take him. Care for him. Hold him. . .

Oh, she'd hold him, all right. Wrap her legs around him and care for him like she'd never cared for anyone before.

"Cole." She meant it as a gentle whisper, but it came out hungry and hoarse.

She had a brief glimpse of his eyes flaring with desire before he crushed her into another kiss. His hand slid up her ribs, grazing her breast just enough to send flames shooting through her soul. But then he yanked away, muttering to himself.

She could sense his inner wolf wrestling for control, though it was still deeply submerged. The battle would turn into full-blown war eventually, but for now, Cole was beating it back. Which gave her hope. If he could keep his balance now, maybe he could hang on to his sanity when the worst of the Change set in.

She grabbed his hand and put it right back where it had been. "I want you to touch me," she whispered. "To want me. To take me."

I want you, her wolf echoed with an inner growl.

The tight muscles of his face relaxed slightly, and she nearly cheered. The inner voice was right; she could help his two sides mesh.

And he can help us, her wolf sighed.

How she and Cole didn't trip over one another, tangoing up those steep stairs, she didn't know. But somehow, they made it to the landing, stepping from blazing sunlight to the shade of the overhanging roof. A place where they could hide from harsh truths for a while.

Cole was the one who kicked the door open, but it was Janna who dragged him inside. She yanked his shirt right over his shoulders the minute they stepped on the braided rug by the door, then got to work on his pants.

"Janna..." he growled in warning.

"I want this." She laughed out of the blue. "It's crazy how much I want this."

"Crazy..." he muttered, cocking his head at her. He shook his head silently, then backed her against a wall. "Crazy enough to want a guy like me?" He squeezed every hard inch of his body against hers and pinned her arms above her head.

She slid a leg around his and reached out for another kiss.

"Wanting you is the only sane part of all this." She didn't expand on *all this*, because explaining was the hard part, but she could get to that later.

Much later, her wolf agreed.

She started the kiss, but he took over and made it all his. Let her know just what kind of loving he'd be subjecting her to. Hard. Fast. Greedy, but indulgent, too, like the way his hands rushed over her breasts, then slowed down to tease and toy.

"Is this shirt a favorite of yours?" he mumbled.

She shook her head breathlessly.

"Good." He tore down the front of it, sending buttons flying. He leaned away just long enough to unclip her bra before pushing forward and capturing her once more.

Mine, his glowing eyes said the second before he dipped down.

Mine, she nearly squeaked, but he sucked a nipple into his mouth, cutting the sound off to a muffled moan.

Mine, mine, mine! she wanted to chant, over and over as he worked her harder, then eased off to scoop the flesh of her breast in his hand. Her all-too-small breast in his all-too-powerful hand, yet it felt just right. So, so right.

She dropped her hands to his head. Tangled her fingers in his hair just the way she'd done in her dreams. Made helpless little kitten sounds as he spread his fingers, letting the nipple peek out just far enough for him to pull it into his mouth and suck.

Then his hands fell away to pop the button on her jeans, and it was just his mouth on her breast. His very capable, very talented mouth, moving from one side to the other.

She thumped her head back against the wall, pushing her chest out. "So good..."

"About to make it better," he murmured out of the side of his mouth.

He slid her jeans and panties down together, freed her from the tangle, and dropped to his knees before her like a penitent man who hadn't worshiped at the right altar for a long, long time.

"Janna..." he murmured, then leaned right in, pushing her legs apart.

She teetered over him. Teetered in every sense of the word as his thumbs spread her slick folds and his tongue slipped in.

The mewing sounds she'd been making went to all-out bordello songs, and she vaguely wished they'd closed the door. But a closed door would have shut out the clean desert air, and that wouldn't be right. Not with her wolf so close to the surface. Not with her dusty cowboy, who seemed a part of the outdoors. A tiny sliver of fresh breeze whispered in, carrying a thousand scents and sounds. The buzz of a bee around the flowers on the sill. The quiet snort of horses in the stables below.

"Cole... Yes... Ah..."

It seemed that every time she tried to communicate how good it felt, he lapped deeper, trapping her words into gridlock that couldn't budge forward or back. Her body was about as useless, too. A good thing for his hands clamped over her hips and the bulk of him parked in front of her boneless limbs.

Cole had two fingers inside her before she knew it, and the dual rhythm of his tongue and the drive inside pushed her closer and closer to the edge. She grabbed his shoulders and let her head roll to the side as her wolf dreamed of a mating bite, and she barely held back her cries as he took her higher... higher...

Cole moved like a man who knew everything about pleasuring a woman and wanted to try it all out on her, A to Z.

"God, Cole," she cried as muscle after muscle clenched. A total meltdown, and he was nowhere near done with her.

"Come for me, Janna," he growled.

"Cole!" she squeaked, then bit her lip to keep the sound from traveling too far. She choked down all the desperate, animal noises building inside until she came with a deep, husky moan. "Cole," she murmured as her knees buckled.

He slid up her body as if commanded — slid easily, like he'd done it all his life. Over her mound, between her breasts, and up along her neck until his chin was tucked over her shoulder and his arms held her tight. His fingers stroked her hair like it was the finest, most exotic silk, and his chest lifted in a sigh.

She'd never felt so cherished. So special. So...renewed.

"Cole..." She guided his chin left and met his lips in a kiss. A kiss that tasted of passion and desire and...and...her. He tasted of her, and just like that, she was on fire again.

"Got a bed in this bunkhouse, cowboy? Or are we going to screw right here on the floor?"

For a second, his look was pure danger that turned on every aching nerve in her body, but then a cheeky cowboy grin came over his face again, and he was all Cole again, all charm.

"Lady's choice."

She laughed. "What if I say both?"

His eyebrows shot up in a surprised look her mind captured and parked among the greatest memories of her life: the most blazing sunsets, the most sidesplitting laughs, the biggest, warmest smiles.

He blinked a little, then grinned. "As you wish, ma'am. As you wish."

Chapter Nine

Cole took a deep breath before Janna nodded him over to the bed, trying to keep himself under control. He'd just about slung her over his shoulder to get her up the stairs, then pulled the rip-her-shirt off stunt that shocked him. Since when did he drag women off onto his turf and tear off their clothes?

But this was one part of impending lunacy he'd be glad to run with as long as Janna was on board with the plan. And man, was she on board.

I want you to touch me. To want me. To take me.

He was a goner the minute she'd spoken the words. They'd hijacked the thinking part of his mind and let instinct take over, and now instinct was taking her to the bed. Not the floor, because somehow, it seemed very, very important to hang on to the last few threads of civilized man left in him. Critical, almost, that he not cross that invisible demarcation line.

So he backed Janna over to the bed and tilted her down, and she went willingly. Enthusiastically. Spreading her long, lean, naked body out under his hungry gaze. Trusting him completely. Which was crazy, because he didn't even trust himself.

"Hey." She smiled, wrapping an ankle around his calf. "Time to lose the jeans."

"I thought you'd never ask."

"I wasn't asking, cowboy." She grinned, making his hard-on even harder.

He slid the jeans off slowly, fighting back his darkest urges. Promising himself he'd keep control of whatever it was inside him that kept trying to grab the reins.

Take her! Claim her! Make her ours!

69

He almost snarled at the voice in the back of his mind. No way. No how. He would make love to Janna the way he wanted to and she agreed with, and no other way.

Show her! Take her! Now! The voice became a roar when her eyes widened at the sight of his hard-on springing free. His nostrils widened, catching the sticky-sweet scent of her desire. The scent threw his mind into the same dizzy spin he'd experienced when he'd first tasted her. Sex used to be all about touch and feel; suddenly, smell and taste were part of it, too. Which might have made him worry if the sensations didn't drive him so wild.

He stepped into the space between her legs, and when she wiggled back and propped her heels on the edge of the bed, exposing herself to him completely, he growled. Really growled, though Janna didn't seem to mind.

I need you, too, her eyes said. Eyes that were wide and wild, but a little worried, too, like they harbored some terrible secret he really, really didn't want to know.

He stood transfixed for a moment, undecided between dropping to his knees to taste her again and prowling over her prone body to nestle his cock at the entrance to her soft folds. Or flipping her over and going at it on all fours, like the voice in the back of his mind kept voting for.

He cocked his head at her. *Lady's choice.*

He didn't say the words aloud, but Janna seemed to know just what he meant.

What if I said all three? her saucy grin asked.

She broke the stalemate a second later by reaching out and pulling him down for a kiss. A deep, greedy kiss she broke a second later with a barely suppressed gasp.

"God, I need you inside me. Now, Cole."

He grinned despite the throbbing ache in his cock.

"You know how often I dreamed about you saying that to me?"

She tilted her chin up, making her hair cascade back. "Really? Dirty dreams? Why, Cole Harper, I didn't think you were the type."

"Then you must not know me very well," he countered.

"No? Then let me get to know you better."

God, it was fun, to go back to the easy banter they'd enjoyed at the start. Before his world upended and everything went askew. He finally felt whole again. Balanced. Complete.

Well, close to complete.

Janna wrapped her legs around him and whispered, "Take me."

The rest came without thinking. He claimed her mouth with a bruising kiss and settled his weight over her body as naturally as though they'd assumed the position a thousand times before. He grabbed a condom from the bedside table, rolled it on, and let his burning cock slide a hard trail down her stomach, across her folds, and finally—

"Cole," she moaned as he thrust in. Deep, deep in, in one hard, hungry slide.

He sucked in a lungful of air and dropped his face to her shoulder, panting there for one silent second.

Will not hurt this woman. Will not hurt her. . .

It became a chant as he pulled back then pushed forward again, relishing her hot, tight hold on him. Relishing the sensation of her body stretching to accommodate him and take him deeper every time.

"Yes. . ." she murmured dreamily. "Yes. . ."

The sticky-sweet scent was strongest at her neck, and he got high on it as he set into a rhythm she met with little bucks of her own.

"Yes. . . Please. . ."

His steady slide became a feverish pound, but Janna just dug her heels into his ass and spurred him on. Gripping the headboard hard, she opened her mouth in silent cries as beads of sweat appeared on her skin. She tilted her hips right and let him scrape along one side of her slick channel, then the other. She spread her legs wider and grazed his back with her nails.

The pinch in his balls became the best kind of about-to-burst agony he'd ever felt, right on the razor's edge of pleasure and pain. He drew her knees over his shoulders, lifting her clear off the bed. Pounded harder and harder, groaning her name.

She mumbled incoherently and swung her head from side to side, drowning him with her heavenly scent. He burrowed against the skin of her neck, and everything in him screamed for him to bite. Janna's body screamed that, too, as she exposed the soft, sinewy flesh of her neck to him.

An artery pulsed in time with his thrusts, and it mesmerized him. Hypnotized him, practically. He reached a hand to her forehead to tip her head even farther back, unable to resist.

Bite her! Claim her! Make her mine!

Temptation. Instinct. Desire. Each wrapped around the other, singing the same song.

Take her! Claim her! Bite!

"Cole," she groaned, exactly at the same time.

He twisted his fingers in her hair and ran the other hand down the line of her neck. Sniffed and found exactly the right spot.

The right spot for what? a distant part of his brain asked.

He had no idea, only that biting her there was what he had to do. What she wanted him to do.

"Yes. . ." Janna mumbled, digging her nails into his back. "Yes. . ."

He spread his jaws wide. Tipped Janna's head even more, then dipped down and scraped his teeth over her throat.

God, that felt good. God, he wanted more.

"Yes. . ." Janna panted so hard, her chest rose and fell.

He nipped at her skin and jolted at the shot of electricity that sent through his soul. If a little nip could do that, a bite would be better, right?

Bite, the inner voice agreed. *Bite deep.*

It was all so dreamy. So intoxicating. So tempting.

"Cole. . ." Janna urged him on.

She was close to coming, as was he, and he wanted nothing better than to bury his cock to the hilt and bite at the same time.

Then Pip barked outside, and both their heads swiveled toward the open door. A momentary distraction that made him gulp.

Holy shit. Had he just been fantasizing about savaging Janna's neck?

He saved the inner lecture for later and tucked his chin a safe distance from her throat. Closing his eyes, he concentrated on finishing what he'd started. Sliding in and out. Reaching deeper and deeper. Letting the windstorm of desire rise inside while he tunneled further into the heaven that was Janna.

"Janna," he croaked. One muscle after another went stiff as he held on, milking his high as long as he could.

"Cole," Janna breathed, shuddering at exactly the same time.

His whole body shook as he came, and a warm wave washed over him. His chin dipped, and he dropped onto her, spent and empty and yet fuller than he'd ever felt. Of love. Of belonging. Of hope.

He closed his eyes and breathed it all in. Pretended there wasn't anything scary about the emotions she unleashed in him. He held her tight against his chest and listened to her heart pound.

"Janna," he whispered, stroking her hair into place. He said it over and over, drowning out the sleepy voice in his head.

Mine, the deep voice mumbled. *Mate.*

Chapter Ten

Janna snuggled closer to Cole, all but purring in contentment.

Wolves don't purr, her inner beast hummed.

She ran a finger down Cole's arm, tracing the cords of muscle that ran this way and that.

Purr, hum, whatever. She felt good.

Real good, her wolf agreed.

"Can I get a rain check for sex on the floor?" she murmured.

When Cole lifted his head to look at her, a long line of muscle stood out along his abdomen. The clouds in his eyes had settled to a warm, calm gray with a golden glow around the edges, like the sun about to peek out from the trailing edge of a winter storm.

"No good?"

She chuckled. "*Too* good. I think I need to spread out my guilty pleasures. You know, like eating chocolate."

"Like what?" The look on his face said he'd never struggled with that particular sin.

She patted his chest and heaved yet another sigh. "Believe me, I want it. Soon."

I want you, my mate. Her wolf nodded along.

His eyes glowed a little brighter, and she wondered if he'd sensed her wolf talking to him. Which would be good, right? Maybe that meant her wolf could help him get through the worst of the Change when the time came.

She glanced at the sunlight slanting in through the open doorway as the sun dipped lower to the horizon. They'd loved their way straight through the afternoon, and night was only a few hours away. Night and the nearly full moon.

Janna opened her mouth. Closed it. Opened it again, fishing for words. She'd come to tell Cole about the Change. To break it to him gently, if such a thing were possible. And here she was, wrapped around him like a horny python around a tree.

But he looked so peaceful, so calm. Calmer than she'd seen him in ages, so she didn't have the heart to say it just yet.

She would, though. She'd tell him soon.

A cool wind whispered through the pines on the mountainside nearby. *Night. Moon. Coming soon.*

She suppressed a shiver by snuggling closer and nuzzling his neck. Nuzzled long and hard until she'd chased the fear and worry away, at least for a little while. Nuzzling was a pleasure nearly as great as sex. Her sister and Simon did a lot of it, and she'd always rolled her eyes at them, but now she knew how they felt. She scraped up against his shoulder, then his neck, rubbing herself in his rich scent. Her wolf made happy, pig-in-mud noises as she did it, and she giggled.

"What?" Cole laughed.

"This. You. Me." She kept right on nuzzling. "Us."

"Us," he echoed.

Us, her wolf sighed, relishing the word. *Finally, we're an us.*

She let out her next breath slowly, because that was the problem. They weren't an *us* yet. Not by a long shot. Somehow, she had to get him through the Change alive. Explain the impossible, then exchange mating bites, and then...

There were about a thousand things that could go wrong along the way, and for a moment, she despaired. But then she pushed the feeling away. Right now, she could enjoy the moment, knowing it helped Cole's inner wolf bond with hers. That was the key.

Well, it seemed like the key. In truth, she knew precious little about what might help a human survive the Change. As a born shifter from a pack in which no one had ever taken a human mate, she really had no clue.

So she went right on nuzzling, because that seemed like the right thing to do.

"You're a champion nuzzler," he chuckled.

If only he knew.

"And you're a champ when it comes to bulls," she ventured. She'd had her heart in her throat, watching him distract the bull earlier that afternoon. The minute she'd made it to the safety of the fence with the little boy, she'd wheeled around and screamed for Cole. Watched him perform crazy, death-defying stunts, like leaping straight over the bull's horns, then ducking under the rear legs when it kicked. He made it look so simple, as if tangling with two thousand pounds of murderous bull was nothing but a game of duck duck goose. The near misses, the instinctive reactions, the level-headed self-control. She'd seen him in action in that television replay, but to see him outfox a bull in real life... Her heart sped up just thinking about it.

Cole made a little sound that said, *If only you knew.*

"How'd you get started with bullfighting?" she asked very quietly, knowing she was venturing onto thin ice.

Cole didn't answer right away. He tightened his arms around her and nuzzled a little more. So long and so pensively, she was about to apologize for asking. But then he spoke.

"My older brothers were into bull riding. Well, calf riding, at first." He chuckled a little, and it didn't even sound forced. "They made me help. We'd set up a little rodeo of our own..."

His voice had a dreamy, once-upon-a-time quality, and she smiled.

"Ha. My sister and I played dress-up when we were little." They also played howl-at-the-moon and catch-the-rabbit, but she wasn't about to mention that. "You guys played rodeo." She shook her head. "How many brothers do you have?"

"Three. And two sisters. One of them played nurse. The other rode bulls, too."

She laughed at the image. "What did your mom think of all that?"

"As long as no one went crying to her, she was more or less okay with it. I think," he added in afterthought.

"Poor woman."

"You have no idea."

She couldn't see his smile from where she lay against his chest, but she could feel it spread inside him.

"I figured I'd end up riding bulls, too, but I stuck with bullfighting. And it was good..."

He trailed off, and she could practically hear the unspoken word: *Until.* She rubbed his chest in circles,

"How'd you get into waitressing?" he blurted, changing the topic, and it sounded so ridiculous, they both laughed.

"Well, I grew up in a family of bartenders, and they made me bring them pretend orders..."

Cole cracked up, and the only thing that kept her from doing the same was the joy of listening to his deep, rich laugh. The kind of free and hearty laugh she wished she could hear all the time.

Maybe we can, her wolf started, hoping against hope.

She rolled and lay on top of Cole, wiggling and grinning like a fool until a horse nickered outside and the real world bumped her conscience once again.

Tell him! part of her pushed. *Tell him now, while he feels good.*

Right. *Cole, I'm a wolf shifter, and you're turning into one, too.*

Like that would work.

You and me, baby, howling at the moon...

Much as her wolf loved the image, she knew that would never fly.

His wolf would like it, though, her inner beast chipped in.

Yes, Cole's inner wolf would like that. But that was the problem. She had to find a way to let the beast out in tiny bits without letting it take control. She'd have to teach Cole's human side to accept the animal within and teach the beast its limits at the same time. Too much, too soon, and the wolf could burst the boundaries of Cole's two sides — literally.

She hid her face in his neck again. Time was running out. The Change was accelerating in Cole. She'd sensed him sniff her neck. Went boneless when he'd nipped her there and practically screamed, *Yes! Yes! Yes!*

78

Thank God she hadn't. A mating bite would drag Cole's beast right to the surface. She had to help him take it slow.

But Jesus, how slow did she dare go? If the beast outpaced her...

She shook her head. Couldn't let that happen. No way could she lose Cole.

His hands played over her back, and she tried concentrating on the human side of her lover. The one still firmly in charge... or so she hoped.

"You know what we should do?" His tone was light and playful.

"What?"

"Go dancing."

"Dancing?" She popped up to examine his face. Was he nuts? She had to save him. Talk to him. Help him through the Change. Dancing was the last thing they ought to do.

"Dancing." He nodded firmly. "Like we did that night."

Janna melted, just thinking about it. The night of their first kiss. A beautiful night, free of worry and doubt. A night that felt light-years away.

Cole ran a gentle finger down her cheek. "Dancing. You and me."

Us. Her wolf nodded eagerly.

Well, maybe it wasn't such a crazy idea. Dancing would let her wolf bond to his a little more, and it would be fun. They could dance for a while, then come back to his place, and she'd tell him once he was good and relaxed.

"Dancing." She nodded. "Good idea."

"Do you have to work tonight?"

She sighed. She ought to be at work already. "Yes."

"Well, I could meet you at the saloon—"

"No!" She cut him off too sharply, then backpedaled. "I mean, how about we meet at Jay's Bar?"

The last thing she needed was for Simon or Soren or her sister to figure out what was happening to Cole. Or worse, for one of the Twin Moon ranch hands to figure it out. They'd drag him straight over to their alpha, and who knew what

79

they'd do next. She'd heard of wolves killing Changelings if they thought madness would set in.

No way was she letting that happen. She had to figure this out alone. Cole needed her — she was sure of it. Her and time and space to make it through the Change. The peace in him came from being with her, because they were destined mates.

My destined mate, her wolf hummed.

He ran a finger along her collarbone and smiled a wicked smile.

"What?"

"You're still naked, you know."

She laughed. "Yeah, well. You're naked, too."

"Convenient," he whispered, and the sound ran a few sensual circles around her ear before sliding deep into her soul.

She cupped his face and kissed him, long and deep and slow, until both their smiles faded to expressions that were more serious. Sensual. She was already draped across his naked body, so it didn't take much for her skin to prickle and heat or for her calm, collected heart rate to speed up.

"Promise you won't buck me off," she murmured, sliding into a straddle over him.

"Promise," he replied, looking up at her as if she were a goddess.

When she leaned back and lowered herself onto his erection, her eyes slid to half-mast and stayed there as she started to rock. And when he reached a hand out to play with her clit, she started squeaking again. Happy little groaning squeaks that made the fire in his eyes dance and flare. Her whole body rode him in long, languid waves, and he pushed up to meet every one.

"So good," she mumbled, breaking into a faster pace. A lope, you might call it, then a wild, out-of-control gallop over bumps and valleys and streams that had her hanging on for her life. "Cole..."

It was the ride of her life — and possibly his, too, judging by how hard he clenched his jaw. His tight grip on her hips might leave bruises, but she didn't care. Not when it kept her anchored tightly against him.

"Yes. . ." She squeezed over him then shuddered, completely out of control.

Cole hissed into a long, raspy groan and released inside her. Hot and sticky and sure to make a mess because they hadn't remembered a condom this time, though she couldn't care less. Not when their connection felt so good. So right.

"Cole. . ." She collapsed over him and clung to him tightly, as if fate might come along any second and pry her away.

"Janna. . ." He wrapped his thick arms around her and hung on in exactly the same way.

Chapter Eleven

Cole knew the bliss of that afternoon had to end sometime, but shoot. Did it have to end so soon?

Showering had still counted among the fun things they'd gotten up to, as did finding something for her to wear afterward.

"Try this one." He'd tossed her a shirt and felt a ridiculous shot of possessive pride when she pulled on his button-down.

"How do I look?" She winked, modeling for him.

You look like mine. My woman. My mate.

The inner voice sounded a lot like the one he spoke aloud with: hoarse. Rumbly. Greedy for more.

"Good. Great."

"You know what I like about you?" she asked out of the blue.

I know what I like about you, he couldn't help thinking.

"What's to like?" He tried keeping the anticipation out of his voice.

She shook her head at that and winched him into another hug. "I think I like everything about you. Especially how well you fit right here." Her fingers played over his back, and she whispered, "I wish I didn't have to go."

He hugged back as tight as he dared. God, he wished, too.

"You'll be okay?" She pulled back as she asked, chewing her lip.

"Fine," he said, wondering if it was a lie. Being with her had brought him a blissful sense of balance. But saying goodbye. . .

He kissed her, then pulled away to get it over with — but didn't quite succeed. He just ended up kissing her again. And again, because letting her go suddenly seemed like a bad idea. She squeezed her body against his, making him warm all over. Hard, too, like this was a greeting and not the parting it had to be.

"Gotta go," she whispered at last, looking sadder than he'd ever seen her.

He held Janna by both arms and stroked her skin for a good minute, trying to soak in enough of her goodness to make it through the rest of the day.

"You okay?" she murmured, cocking her head to blink at him through her doe eyes.

"Good." Looking at her, how could he feel any other way?

"Jess will be waiting," she murmured, more to herself than to him.

Yeah, he was a greedy bastard, because he wanted her all to himself. But she had a job, just like he did, and it was time to let go.

He forced himself to release her, one reluctant finger at a time, and tried to muster a grin. "See you soon?"

She nodded. Quickly, enthusiastically. "Tonight?"

Janna had a way of saying the word that made him shiver in the very best way.

"Tonight." He nodded.

"Jay's Bar," she said, and then she was off. Every step she took put a crack in his heart, and he shuffled a few steps closer to her car.

Mine! Mate!

"You sure you'll be okay?" she called, like he was a kid being left home alone for the first time.

It felt like that, too.

"Fine." He nodded and said it over and over again as she drove away.

He kicked the dirt and studied his boots for a little while before tilting his head back at the pure blue sky, streaked with the first pink hues of sunset. As beautiful as Janna. Well, almost. She was more beautiful than any view. More beautiful than the whole of Arizona, and that was saying a lot. More beautiful than—

84

He kicked the dirt again and sighed. Yeah, she was beautiful, all right. And perfect. So perfect for him.

"Excuse me," an uncertain voice called.

He turned and saw a woman he didn't recognize, approaching him with a child in tow.

"We wanted to thank you..." she said.

Right — the mother of the child who'd run into the bull pen. The little guy was at her side, hiding something behind his back while his shy eyes stayed firmly rooted to the ground.

"Come on, Johnny," the lady said. "Give it to the nice man."

Cole didn't know if it was him scaring the kid or the situation, but either way, it seemed like a good idea to squat down.

"Hey," he tried.

The little boy looked at his mother, who gestured to Cole. Eventually, the kid stuck a piece of paper in front of Cole's nose.

"Now what do we have here?" Cole asked, taking it.

"A picture," the boy whispered, dragging a foot in the dirt.

Cole turned the paper around, studied the jumble of lines and blobs, and whistled. "Nice picture. Did you draw this?"

He had no idea what was drawn under the crooked words THANK YOU, but it seemed like the right thing to say.

The boy nodded.

"There's the bull." The mother pointed, acting as art interpreter.

Cole tilted his head. Yeah, that U-shape could be horns.

"Big bull," he murmured.

"And there you are," the mother said, pointing to what appeared to be a stick figure. A really tall stick figure that seemed to dwarf the bull.

"Wow. I'm big, too."

He meant it as a joke, but the kid moved his head in a series of jerky nods. "Really big," he breathed.

Cole hid a smile behind the back of his hand.

"And there's Johnny," the mom finished.

Another little stick figure stood on the side beside a couple of lopsided smiley faces that had to be the parents.

Cole looked at it for a good, long time. Cleared his throat a couple of times, because all of a sudden he was all dry and scratchy inside.

"Well, thanks," he said, standing up quickly. "I think I have a great place for this picture."

"Thank you," the mother said. Her voice was quiet, but the gratitude in her eyes just about screamed out loud. Then she took the little boy's hand and turned back toward the house.

Cole stood there a while longer, looking at the dust settle on the road, then at the picture. Closed his eyes and looked at memories for a while, too. Good memories. Bad ones. Everything in between. Then he took a deep breath and looked up again, wishing Janna were around to put it all in words for him. Even if she didn't say anything, she'd have that *I get it* look he wished he could see right now.

Then he strode to the stables, because a guy couldn't stand and stare at an empty stretch of road all day. He dropped the picture off at his apartment — a place that felt twice as small and four times as empty now that Janna was gone — then went to the stables. The horses tossed their heads and nickered warily but settled down and let him work. Pip came over, looking strangely meek, too. The dog kept his tail between his legs and licked Cole's hand like he'd been granted an audience with the Pope or a king.

Something inside him gave a grunt of satisfaction. *Top Dog. Me. The boss.*

Which was ridiculous, because all the animals knew Rosalind was the big boss. That had always been okay with him, as long as he came a close second. But tonight...something had shifted somehow. Even Thunder, who nipped anyone who came into his stall, didn't pull any of his usual tricks.

Cole swept the center of the barn, then leaned against the creaky door. The stars had come out, one by one, and hung winking in the indigo sky. Crickets chirped and warm yellow light radiated from Rosalind's place and the guest house nearby. The scent of stew carried on the dry air, and he breathed it in deep.

Peace. Goodness. Harmony. It was in the slopes of the hills, in the quiet murmur of the animals in the barn. A firefly blinked on and off, not far from Cole's knee.

A nice night. A good night. With more goodness to come because he had a date with Janna. He had plenty of time to get cleaned up for her, and he'd do a good job because he cared for a change.

He headed back to his place and ate some leftovers. Looked around and swore, because damn, it was a mess, and Janna might come over later. So he set about cleaning and tidying — for a whole hour since he had time to kill. But the cleaner he got the place, the more off-balance he felt.

He showered again, trying to scrub the feeling away, but it only got worse. His gut clenched up, not from the food but from the feeling inside. He shaved slowly, carefully, pretending everything was fine.

He turned and checked his back in the mirror, looking for a reminder of Janna. She'd scratched his back enough to have cooed over it afterward, which he'd enjoyed almost as much as he'd enjoyed the act that had created the scratches in the first place.

He twisted and craned his head over his shoulder. Not a scratch in sight. All gone. All healed. That fast?

An hour after he'd shaved, he ran his hand over his chin and crap, he'd missed several patches, so he started all over again. He really ought to get a better light because he kept overlooking spots. That, or the stubble kept speeding right back in again.

His arm itched — ferociously — and his mood soured. Could he not enjoy half a day of happiness without the constant ups and downs?

He fiddled around the place for another hour, getting more and more restless, until he finally stormed out the doorway and onto the landing, just to have someplace to stomp to. He grabbed the handrail and gritted his teeth against the pain under his nails. That nails-being-pulled-out feeling again.

Then his chin snapped up to the night sky, and he froze.

The moon shone on him like a spotlight, and he threw up a hand to block it.

"Goddamn moon," he cursed under his breath.

Cursing felt better than fretting about nothing, so he said it again. "Goddamn moon."

He shook his fist at it and repeated the words until he was babbling like a crazy man and the letters slurred. The part he held longest was the A of *damn* and the long OO of *moon*. A. Moon. Mooooon. A. Ooooon. A... Ooooo...

Before he knew it, a howl rose up in his mind.

Aroooooo.

A strangled, angry sound that his body wanted to sway with, like a dance.

Aroooooo...

He darted inside and slammed the door so hard, the windows rattled in their panes. Then he backed up until he dropped to the bed and slammed his hands over his eyes.

Think about Janna. Think about good things.

He tried, but the *good* kept meandering off into *bad*. Like how desperately he'd wanted to tear into her neck. What kind of sick mind thought up things like that?

Mate. Needs us. Wants us, the dark voice said.

He shook his head and ground his molars. Freeze-framed back to the glorious image of Janna riding him. Her pert little breasts had swayed with the rest of her body, and her glossy hair had danced back over her shoulders. She'd leaned over him with a hot, hungry look, and her hair tickled his skin. So shiny and fine, his fingers reached into thin air.

But no Janna. Not for real. Just images that got worse and worse. Images he feared might become real.

Like Janna screaming, not in passion but in pain. In fear. He saw hands all over Janna, ripping her clothes. Raping, pillaging hands that reared back and rushed forward with merciless slaps and punches.

"Janna!" he cried aloud, and the sound carried into the night.

Cole! Her mouth opened and closed as she screamed in the terrible vision. Was she screaming at him? For him? He couldn't tell.

Mine. Must have her! Must have my mate! the voice went crazy inside.

Stop! Janna screamed. *Stop!*

But he didn't stop, and the images got worse. It was him, hurting her. The realization made him sick. He'd ripped her shirt off that afternoon. He'd eyed her neck. Now this crazy moon fever was upon him, and he wanted to do worse.

Must get to her...

He jumped up and bolted the door. Dragged the desk in front of it, too. He hunched as he did it, because his back was bowed and bent.

Will not hurt Janna! Never.

The banging in his head became an earsplitting screech, and the ugly images got even worse. Janna, screaming. Fighting. Losing...

Whatever force had taken over his mind made him roll to all fours and snap his head up toward the door.

Get Janna! Find her! Now! the voice barked.

He scrambled backward, fighting madly. Promising himself he would not break through the door and heed that evil voice.

Claim her!

He fought it every step, but the body that was not quite his own inched closer to the door while he fought and shouted inside.

No! No! No!

Out of the jumble of wild images that bombarded him, one jumped to the foreground. Janna, leaning forward and handing him her bandana. Saying, *Hang on to this.* Kissing him.

Hang on to this...

A thousand more images flashed, and the pain grew worse.

His fingers groped empty air, suddenly desperate for that bandana. Where the hell was it?

The bandana was gone, but he remembered the kiss.

Hang on to this...

So he hung on to that memory with everything he had. Let his mind push back the pain and the awful banging and greedy voice in his mind. He concentrated on the memory of her soft lips. Her rose-petal tongue. Her hands, flat on his chest. The tickle of her breath as she tasted him and let him taste her back. A taste like raspberry muffin and sweet iced tea, mixed with something just a little bit wild.

He hung on to the kiss for dear life and added nuzzling to the image, too. He stumbled toward the bed, panting. Remembering Janna spread out there, so eager for him. So innocent, so undeserving of anything but love.

His body was on fire. His shoulder blades pinched backward, and his skin itched all over, the way it used to do on that one spot on his arm. His jaw swung open in a shout of pain but no sound came out. Worse, his jaw locked in that position. It stretched much farther than it should until the skin on his face stretched, too, and became a mask. A twisted, horrible mask his hands flew over frantically, finding everything in the wrong place. A long, protruding nose. High, pointed ears. Stubble, not just on his chin but everywhere.

Arizona was full of old native legends about demons and devils that he'd never paid attention to. He writhed on the floor, wondering if he ought to have. Wondering if there was any way to save his body or his mind.

His fingers tensed up and clawed the air, and bolts of pain sparked through his body. He'd broken plenty of bones in his time, but now it was happening all at once, and all over. Even his mind started to blur.

Then everything tipped sideways, and he crashed to the floor.

Chapter Twelve

"Four ball in the corner pocket," Janna murmured, lining up her shot.

Click! The balls rolled across the green felt of the pool table, bounced exactly as she'd intended, and the four ball made a satisfying plonk into the corner pocket.

Someone whistled. "Nice shot."

She didn't take her eyes off the pool table, nor her mind from where it really was: Cole. What to do, how to do it.

Part one of her plan had come off without a hitch, thank goodness. She'd endured what seemed like the longest evening shift of her life at the saloon then headed out, telling her sister the truth. Well, most of the truth, like where she was going. She did embellish a little by saying four guys from Twin Moon Ranch would be there, too. In reality, the last thing she needed was a chaperone for the night — and definitely not four shifter chaperones who'd take one look at Cole and cry wolf.

Her eyes darted to the door of Jay's Bar for the hundredth time in the last twenty minutes, then went back to the pool table to calculate her next shot. Some people took long walks to clear their minds. Her sister needed to bake. Janna played pool.

"Six ball, side pocket," she said, taking aim.

A couple of guys had clustered around the table, but she barely paid attention to them. They were part of the background, like the country music, the clink of glasses, the stale smell of beer. Funny how the first time she'd been here, she didn't pick up on what a dive the place really was. Her eyes had been focused on Cole's sandy hair. Her nose, filled with his oaky scent. Her mind, whirring with possibilities.

Now her mind just spun. She'd done all the subtle questioning she could do at the Blue Moon, but all she'd learned was what she already knew: how low the survival rate for Changelings really was.

Shit, shit, shit.

Her mind made up a dozen reasons why none of that applied to Cole. Her mate was strong. Smart. And he had her to help him, right?

Which is exactly what she'd do. She'd talk to him. Try to explain. Then she'd bring him to Tina Hawthorne-Rivera, because she'd concluded she really did have to enlist some help. Tina would know what to do. Tina's own mate had survived the Change, so Cole could, too. It would all be fine. Somehow, everything would work out.

When the bar door opened, she straightened in hope, but the man who walked in was a leather-jacket toting, trucker type.

Damn it, where was Cole?

"Looks like your date ain't coming," the guy nearest her said in a flat tone.

"Got lots of good company here, though." A second grinned.

Janna leaned over the table for a tricky kick shot, ignoring them. Okay, maybe meeting at Jay's Bar hadn't been such a good idea. The minute Cole showed up, she was out of here.

But when the music playing over the speakers switched, she went warm all over. Started swaying with it, too, because it was the very song she and Cole had first danced to, and she could still feel the tickle of him whispering the words in her ear.

There's songs and poems and promises, and dreams that might come true. . .

That dance had been a high, and the slower song that followed led to their first kiss. A kiss that had her knees knocking. She closed her eyes and replayed it in her mind. Such soft lips for such a hard-toned man. Such a clean, woodsy scent, like home. Such a gentle hand, on her waist. . .

A hand really did slide over her waist then, nowhere near as gently as Cole's, and she smacked it away.

"Watch it," she barked, whipping around to swing her pool stick toward the man who'd snuck up behind her.

Yeah, watch it, asshole, her wolf snarled inside.

She glared, finding a different man than before. Her nostrils flared, but all she could smell on the guy was a weird, whiskey-laced-with-diesel scent.

The man backed off as his beefy friends chortled all around. "Sorry, honey."

She made a face and turned back to the pool table. Couldn't a woman just be left alone to think for a while?

A breath of fresh air came wafting down a short hallway where someone had propped open the bar's back door, letting in just enough of the cool night to make things bearable.

She pursed her lips. Next time she decided to meet Cole somewhere, it would be a nicer place than this dive.

She concentrated on the layout of balls around the table and calculated her next shot. What she needed was a good, three-ball shot to settle her mind a bit.

"Two ball in the side pocket," she muttered, bending over again.

"No way," one of the men said.

Watch this, her wolf growled.

She sent the eight ball hurtling down the middle of the table, where it struck the seven in a glancing blow that, in turn, sent the two ball rolling through a tight gap into the side pocket.

Plonk. The two ball fell away.

Janna stalked around the table, completely ignoring the applause of the men around her. One of them brushed up against her, and she immediately stepped away. Jesus, could they just let her think?

Obviously, she needed a new game plan for how to go about things when Cole showed up, because Jay's Bar didn't have the cozy atmosphere she remembered from before. Next time, she'd take Cole to a diner. Better yet, on a picnic in the mountains. Anything would be better than this.

93

"Wanna dance, sweetheart?" a voice said, much too close to her ear.

She sighed and glanced toward the bar out of habit, half expecting to see Simon there. Bears were handy that way — one glare from him and these idiots would back away from her. But of course, it wasn't Simon, because this wasn't the Blue Moon Saloon.

The bartender here was a pudgy, balding guy who didn't keep an eye on things the way Simon and Soren did. Something she'd never appreciated until just now. She'd never had an issue waitressing in the saloon because the guys kept things in line. But this place...

She looked around. Trucker types. Bikers. Lots of tattoos. Mostly men, too, which she hadn't noticed before.

Whatever. That didn't worry her. Even if the men closest to her got rowdy, they were only human. Nothing her wolf couldn't handle if push came to shove. The only thing she had to worry about was Cole.

She circled to the corner of the table nearest the wall and bent, lining up her next shot. She could go for the three ball, over there, or a trickier shot with the five ball and set up her next shot...

"How about a dance, honey?"

She stuck out an elbow, undeterred. "Not your honey. Five ball in the—"

She yelped as two thick, tattooed arms grabbed her from behind. Really grabbed her, pinning her arms to her sides and her back to his front.

"I think a dance is just what this wildcat needs," he chuckled, prying the pool stick out of her hand. His beer breath washed over her ear.

She opened her mouth to scream, then thought the better of it. All she needed was to stomp on his foot, then twist to the right and elbow him in the gut. That always worked.

So she stomped and twisted, but it didn't work. The man was quicker than anticipated and clutched her harder.

"How about you and me head outside for some fun?" he said, pulling her toward the door.

"Stop! Stop!" she protested.

Two other men closed around them, blocking the view of anyone who might look over and protest while the blaring music covered her cry.

Janna struggled, cursing herself. She'd been stupid, coming to this bar alone. Working under the watchful eye of two bears had made her complacent. Well, fine. Let these jerks get her into the alley outside. She could use the darkness to let her wolf claws out and give them a whipping to remember. No one would believe a couple of half-drunk rowdies who'd claimed to have seen a woman turn wolf.

She stopped struggling and flexed her fingers, getting ready to call on her inner beast.

"That's right, sweetie," the man at her ear chuckled. "Come along and meet our friends."

Friends? Her heart pounded in her chest. What friends?

The three men had her boxed in the narrow hallway. There was no way anyone in the bar would spot her. Forward was her only way out — into the alley.

She took a deep breath, trying to keep calm. Fighting off two or three drunks, she could do. But any more than that and things would get ugly. She'd have to shift fully to wolf form and tear out a few throats. She'd still get away, but it would bring unwanted attention to the incident. Injuries and bodies would lead to an investigation that could threaten the secrecy shifters valued above all else.

Her heart sank. Even if she managed to cover things up, there was only so much trouble the wolves of Twin Moon Ranch would tolerate from the likes of her and her sister, who were technically guests in pack territory. They'd be cast out. Their jobs, their new home — she and Jessica could lose everything.

Shit. Her only choice was to get away quickly without hurting any of the men badly enough to warrant attention. And damn, would that leave a bitter taste in her mouth. These jerks deserved the worst. Who knew how many other women they'd try helping themselves to in the future?

Another wave of garlic breath washed over her face, and she turned away, counting the steps to the back door. The second they were outside, she'd shift and run.

"Right this way, sweetheart..."

Oh, she'd show him *sweetheart*, all right.

"Hang on, Lou," one of the others said, and all of a sudden, the hands gripping hers twisted and yanked.

She yelped at the pain.

"Perfect," the man pronounced a moment later, pushing her shoulders.

She yanked her hands apart the second he let go, but her arms didn't budge.

Shit!

No matter how she twisted or pulled, she couldn't get her hands free. They kept catching on something...

"I think she likes your belt," the first man chuckled.

Belt? They'd tied her hands with a belt?

Panic rose in her, and she barely batted it down. Jesus, now what? She couldn't shift with her hands tied behind her back. Both shoulders would be dislocated, and even a quick-healing wolf couldn't recover instantly from that.

Shit... shit...

She bit her lip, closed her eyes, and reached for her sister in her mind. It took a huge gulp to swallow away her pride, but this wasn't about pride any more.

Jess! she screamed inside. *Help! Please!*

Even if her sister heard, she couldn't teleport over. By the time help arrived...

Janna struggled again, fighting the ugly images in her mind.

"Now, now, sweetheart. You just keep on walking along. 'Cause those friends of ours? They're your friends, too. Old friends."

Old friends? What old friends would cooperate with men like these to rape her?

The man pushed her out the back door, and she had half a second to breathe the cooler night air before stumbling into another man who had been waiting outside. She lurched aside, but there was a third one there, clad all in white.

"Janna Macks," he said coolly. "Such a pleasure to see you again."

"You," she blurted.

The man smiled and waved her captors away with a hundred dollar bill. "We'll take it from here, boys."

Janna backed away. The three men who'd hauled her outside were one thing. But this...this new enemy put ice in her blood.

Even in the dim light of the alley, she could make out the blue rings tattooed on their fingers. Blue Bloods. The rogue band who'd murdered her family and attacked the saloon not long before. Five of them.

"Seems you still haven't learned your lesson." Victor Whyte, the leader of the Blue Bloods, shook his head sadly. Then his face twisted into one of sheer malice. He grabbed her hair and twisted it, forcing her to her knees. "We're here to teach you. The hard way."

He pulled her head back — so far back, she could see the moon overhead. So far back, it was a wonder her neck didn't snap.

God, he was going to kill her here. Now.

"You said we'd get a chance to play with her first," one of the rogues gathered in the alley protested.

Play? She winced. She'd rather die quickly than endure what they had in mind.

She yanked at the belt tying her hands and felt it give slightly. If she could stall for a few minutes, she might be able to get it off. But Jesus, she didn't have minutes. She had seconds, at best.

She drew in a huge gulp of air and screamed into the night. Drawing help — any help — was her only chance.

The big man behind her smacked his hand over her mouth a second too late, and they all stood, listening for a reaction for a moment or two.

"We kill her," the leader hissed. "Now—"

He turned at the sound of hurried footsteps pounding into earshot. A tall figure appeared at the end of the alley, silhouetted by a dim streetlight.

97

Janna's hope sparked, then faded. There was only one man there, not the armed posse she'd been praying for. An innocent man who'd likely be killed, too. God, what had she done?

"Hey!" he shouted, and everyone froze.

Janna looked up, recognized him, and blurted one hopeless word.

"Cole?"

Chapter Thirteen

Cole stood panting much harder than he ought to have been for the short run from his pickup to the alley. But he'd been panting the whole drive over. Pulling on his collar, too, and gnashing his teeth, not to mention scratching his ear so hard, it hurt. The urgency had been enough to pull him back from the abyss he'd been about to career over and run to his car. Trying desperately to keep the madness at bay just long enough to... to what, he wasn't so sure. Only that he had to push the beast he was turning into back and get to Janna right away.

"Back off!" he yelled. Much as he wanted to sprint down the alley and punch their dirty hands off her, he went slowly, checking the scene.

Four — no, five — big guys. He couldn't see their faces but his nose caught a bleachy, unnatural scent that made him snort for clean air.

The warning bells that had been clamoring in his mind on the way over went off on a second frenzied round.

"You," he huffed, recognizing the man who'd led the attack on Janna in the saloon weeks ago. The man he'd confronted once before.

He bared his teeth and a low growl filled the alley. A real, animal growl that would have scared him if he'd stopped to think.

Let me out! a gritty voice yelled from inside. *Kill them! Kill!*

Killing, he had no problem with. Not with guys who dragged a woman into an alley and tied her up. But it was the same voice that had been screaming at him to do all kinds of crazy things to Janna, and he wasn't about to let it take control.

His facial muscles twitched wildly as he scratched an ear like a lunatic. Yes, he was going crazy. A fucking Dr. Jekyll, Mr. Hyde he was powerless to control.

"Cole! Don't!" Janna called.

He'd have jumped off a cliff for her. But desert her when she was in danger? No way.

Four of the five guys were big and burly, and the fifth was a pudgy older guy who spoke like he goddamn owned the place.

"We've got everything under control here. No need to get mixed up in other people's business."

Right, under control. Cole almost spat the words aloud, but his jaw was killing him. That feeling of teeth being push-pulled again, all four canines at the same time.

He shook his head and advanced another step, balling his fists.

The man had white hair and wore a white suit that seemed completely out of place in a dank alley at night. Whyte, that was the asshole's name. He tilted his head at Cole and his eyes lit up in recognition.

"Ah, our knight in shining armor, back for another try."

More like a raging bull, but whatever. Let the guy bullshit all he wanted.

Shift! Shift! Let me out!

Cole had no idea what the inner voice meant by *shift*, but he sure as hell wasn't letting another enemy loose in the alley right now.

You need me to save her!

No way. He had to keep a cool head. To figure out a way to fight five guys long enough to let Janna get away.

The two men holding Janna started backing away with Whyte, while the two men closest to him stepped forward. For a moment, he could still see Janna, watching in desperation, and the next, a big body stepped between them, blocking his view.

Which was when the plan to keep cool went out the window.

100

Cole lowered a shoulder and charged the first guy. Rammed hard enough to send the ass sprawling then turned just in time to avoid the second guy's fist. He caught the outstretched arm and twisted it hard, making the man grunt and drop to his knees.

He did it without thinking, and thank God, because the inner voice was screeching now.

Let me out! Let me kill them!

"Move," Whyte barked, and the man holding Janna dragged her backward. When she dug in her heels, he slapped her.

Cole winced at Janna's pained cry and blinked at the dejá vu. Janna, fighting off hands that slapped and grabbed at places no man had a right to touch, not when a woman didn't want him to.

It hadn't been him hurting Janna in his nightmares. It was these men.

His vision went red with fury, and he took his vengeance on the next guy with a vicious left hook. The guy stumbled for his footing while Cole paused to cradle his right hand. Jesus, he might as well have punched a brick wall. But the pain in his hand was nothing compared to the searing pain in his mind. Like his brain was being drawn and quartered. Torn by a hundred impulses and instincts, all contradicting each other. The voice in his head was winning control over his body, making his arm twitch, his lips draw back. He started snarling — not just on the inside, but on the outside, too, like a rabid dog.

Stay in control. Stay in control...

Give me control! the wild thing demanded. *Give it to me! I'll save her!*

"Cole!" Janna yelled.

He looked up just in time to sidestep the man jumping at him. He spun and booted the man into the trash cans standing by the wall. The other men stirred into action behind him, making inhuman noises as they did. There was a bone-chilling popping sound, along with a guttural moan. Clothing ripped, maybe catching on something as they rolled to their feet. He

101

heard a growl and a furry kind of rattle, too, like a dog shaking itself. The scent of musky dog — the kind Rosalind's car was filled with — reached him, making the hair on the nape of his neck rise.

The ringleader in that ridiculous white suit glanced behind Cole and smirked.

"Fight us now, cowboy." He nodded at the others. "Try fighting us now."

"Run, Cole," Janna whispered, going wide-eyed. "Run now!"

No way would he run. He'd face them like a man and go at them again. And again, and again, for as long as it took until Janna was safe.

You run, he telegraphed with his eyes. *The second you can get away, run.*

He turned, raising his fists, and pulled up short, because there was no one behind him. No one at eye level, anyway.

A hellish snarl rose out of the quiet of the night, and he looked down.

What the...

Three big dogs gnashed their ivory teeth at him, drooling saliva. Their scrappy fur bristled along their backs and their eyes gleamed.

Not dogs. Wolves. Where did they come from?

The second he thought it, his body convulsed. His elbows shot up and back, and he bent double like he'd been punched in the stomach. All the color seeped out of his vision until all that was remained was black, white, and a thousand different grays.

They came from inside. Just like me, the voice in him snarled. *Let me out!*

He choked on his own breath. No way was he letting any such beast loose. He'd die before he did that.

Trust me.

Trust his own crazy mind? Trust a beast that wanted to hurt Janna?

I will never hurt her! The voice clawed at him from the inside, splitting his mind. His fingers flexed of their own accord,

102

and his shoulders convulsed backward. So hard, the pain was more color — white — than sensation, and he fell to his knees.

"Cole," Janna cried. "Let it out! Quick!"

He knew the wolves were advancing on him, but he didn't understand how Janna knew about the voice inside him.

Let him help me, she said. The strange thing was, her voice didn't reach his ears. It was all in his mind. *Let your wolf out!*

He didn't have a wolf. He had a fucking headache, three wolves about to rip his throat out, and not a second to spare.

Trust it! Janna cried.

This time, her words came with images that rushed into his splintered mind. Some pleasant, like that meadow in the mountains, where he'd dreamed of grass tickling his nose while he padded along on the ground. Other images were brutal but empowering, like the snap of mighty jaws. The liberating feel of four legs, the sheer power he could possess...

You can do it!

A wolf. She wanted him to turn into a wolf, like these murderous beasts?

Not like them. You'll see. Now! Shift now!

If he could choose to turn into any animal, it would be a bull. That, he understood. The way to move, to turn, to kick. To seek with his horns. He could do a bull. But a wolf?

I'm your only chance! the gritty voice inside him said. *Janna's only chance!*

Shift! Janna screamed as the three wolves closed on him. *Damn it, shift now!*

The order zipped through his body and mind, and he had no choice but to surrender. His shoulders pulled back and his jaw gave way to the scratching pain of lengthening teeth and cracking bones.

I'm your partner, not your enemy, stupid. Let me out!

Let it out! Janna echoed.

Cole closed his eyes and conjured up his own image of that mountain meadow, in which Janna was just in front of him, swishing her tail...

He opened his eyes just in time to roll out of the way of the nearest wolf's snapping jaws. He jumped to his feet and

103

launched himself at it, baring his jaws. It was only in midleap that he registered the fact that he'd jumped off four feet, and that his nose was a long way in front of his eyes. No time to question that, though. Not in the thick of the fight.

He tore into the wolf's neck then jumped away as the other two closed in.

They growled, and he growled back. A real growl, vibrating in a deep, curved chest, and it felt good. Powerful. Mighty, even, and mighty pissed off.

The three wolves circled him, snarling the whole time. Checking him out just long enough for him to take stock, too.

Four feet and a goddamn tail... attached to him. A mind aflame with fury and a blazing need to kill. All totally foreign, but the soul inside... that still felt like his.

I am you, stupid, the voice muttered, echoing inside him as if he'd whispered the words to himself.

Me?

He shook his head and felt a pair of ears flap around his face. Jesus, it was true. The wolf was him. And it wasn't a raging beast that would hurt Janna in the worst possible way. The beast would protect her to the bitter end.

So let's get started, it said.

Cole nodded and snarled at his foes. *Yes. Let's.*

Chapter Fourteen

Janna stared as Cole shifted from man to wolf, as shocked and mesmerized as a human would be upon seeing a were shift in front of their eyes. Not because she'd never witnessed a shift but because of what it might mean in Cole's case. Death? Madness? The end?

In all the time she'd spent worrying about this moment, she'd imagined a slow, agonizing shift. A foaming mouth and wild eyes, signaling the battle within. Groans of excruciating pain and a clumsy, awkward change.

She should have known Cole could do better than that.

He shifted the way he'd tangoed with the bull: seamlessly. Gracefully. One second, he was standing as sure and fierce as any a cowboy ever had, and the next...the fairest, sleekest wolf she'd ever seen burst into a series of furious attacks. Quick and agile, with the same sense of perfect timing he had as a man. He rolled away from his attacker, then twisted and snapped back. Turned on the other rogues and kept pace as they snarled and circled him.

"Whoa," the man holding Janna muttered.

"Get him!" Victor Whyte snapped at the three rogues who had shifted into wolf form.

Janna used the distraction to jerk free. She stumbled back and landed hard on her ass, but her wrists shifted within their bounds. A little more slack and she'd be able to—

"Watch her!" Whyte barked.

When the fifth man hauled her up by the elbow, the belt cut into her wrists. She winced away the pain and focused on extending one wolf claw. A single claw and nothing else — a tricky operation so unlike her usual all-or-nothing shift.

The alley exploded into a frenzy of growls and barks as the three rogues pounced on Cole.

"Cole!" she screamed.

For a minute, all she saw was a tangle of fur and fangs. Then Cole leaped free, jumping toward her, with his golden fur stained burgundy. God, was that his blood or the blood of the enemy?

The three rogues whirled, forming a line, and Cole turned his back on Janna to face them. He snarled a warning any wolf in a ten-mile radius would have heard.

Mine! Mate!

She didn't know whether to cry or to cheer. The snarl indicated that Cole had accepted the wolf half of himself — but at what cost? If he ceded too much control to the wolf, his human side might be lost forever.

Janna sawed frantically at the edge of the leather with her claw.

One rogue feinted, and Cole batted him back with a huge, outstretched paw. A second rogue seized the chance to snap at Cole's back leg, but Cole was faster. He jumped out of the way then spun and leaped at the rogue, who yelped and darted away.

Janna shook her head. Three against one meant all Cole could do was shake each attack off. He could never move in to kill a single wolf, because the other two would close in.

"I'll take her. You get him," Whyte ordered the man guarding her.

Shit. Four against one. She sawed faster.

Whyte started dragging her backward. His hands were cold and clammy on her bare skin.

"Should have learned your lesson a long time ago," he hissed in her ear.

His breath was foul; his tone haughty.

"Purity," he crowed. "Purity..."

The words brought her to the night her pack had been ambushed and annihilated by Whyte's rogues. Simon and Soren had hunted down and killed all those directly responsible, but they were just the tip of the iceberg. Whyte had been the one who'd incited the attack. And he would order attacks on more innocent shifters if he wasn't stopped.

She sawed desperately at the belt as four wolves battled Cole in a messy, merciless fight.

She was ready to scream in frustration when the belt broke, and she was suddenly free. Her hands flew apart, immediately formed fists, and punched the rogue leader in the face.

"Bitch!" he yelled, stumbling back.

Janna summoned the other four claws and slashed at Whyte again. The rip of bare flesh under her claws had never felt so satisfying.

"Bitch this." She snarled, dropped to all fours, and shifted into her wolf form.

Whyte shrank back, and it took everything she had not to go for his throat. She couldn't afford to let the coward go, but even a second spent attacking him might be a second too late for Cole. She wheeled away from Whyte and snarled at the rogues in the fight.

Mate! Save my mate! her wolf cried as Cole went down.

Four rogues closed over him, going for the kill.

Janna leaped forward, tackling the nearest rogue. She chomped down on his ear, pulling him to the side. The male wolves had a size advantage, but surprise was on her side. Surprise, fury, and a crushing need for revenge. She dove at his throat and closed down hard.

Die, enemy. Threaten my mate and you die, her wolf snarled.

His blood was acrid, his matted fur dank. She held on as he struggled. This one would die. The next one would die, too. All of them, even if it meant her own death.

She spat when the rogue went still and focused on finding Cole. The fight between him and the rogue wolves had gone from a pileup to a three-on-one triangle again. For a split second, she caught Cole's eye and cried into his mind.

Cole?

Janna! His husky voice sounded in her head. A voice just enough like the real Cole to give her hope.

107

She wanted to take him by the shoulders and shake him until she could be sure his human side wasn't slipping away, but there was no time. The rogue closest to her pivoted and barreled straight at her.

She borrowed a page from Cole's bullfighting book and sidestepped at the last second, then bit down on the rogue's back leg. The wolf kicked madly as chaos broke out beside her: two versus one in the other fight.

Better odds than before, her wolf decided.

It was up to her to make the odds even better, so she hung on as her foe dragged her along. The wolf was a big one, so she dug her claws into the ground, trying to make him stumble. Looking for an opening—

There! She clawed at his belly and slashed a deep gash.

"Get them! Get them!" Whyte yelled from a safe distance.

Janna let go of the rogue's leg and hurtled herself at his neck. She snapped just short of flesh and closed on the loose skin — a painful, but not mortal blow, damn it. She released him, and the rogue scrambled away, looking at her with wide, white eyes.

Janna had never felt bigger. Braver. More frightening. But she was frightened, too. How badly was Cole injured? How deep was his soul buried under the wolf's?

Two wolves bellowed behind her, and one howled. She turned, frantic to identify which had been wounded.

Not Cole. Please, not Cole...

A rogue limped to the left, giving up the fight.

"Get back, you coward!" Whyte shouted.

She'd never been so tempted to jump for the injured one and kill in cold blood. But the fight wasn't over, and she couldn't lose her focus on Cole. He and the biggest rogue reared up on their hind legs and wolf-wrestled before crashing sideways. They broke apart, roaring, and then came together again.

Janna watched for her chance to catch the big one off guard. One of the rogues was dead, another limping away. Whyte kept a safe distance from the action, posing no immediate threat. She did the math quickly. That left one more rogue — the one she'd bitten and clawed. She turned just in time to see him coming at her with his teeth bared. It was too late to react, and she went flying. The rogue leaped in for the kill as she floundered on her back, trying to scramble back to her feet. The second she did, she attacked with everything she had: claws, teeth, and the pounding need to avenge her family. She drove the rogue right back against the wall, where he finally turned and ran.

Panting wildly, Janna looked for Cole. She heard a snap, a gurgling cry, then near-silence but for the pulsing beat of the music coming from the bar. The wolf standing victorious over a dead foe was so bloodstained, she couldn't tell which it was.

Cole? The rogue? Who? She screamed inside. Who?

Then their eyes met, and she knew.

Cole?

Janna? His eyes were dark, his face drawn and confused.

Two rogues were dead, and two others slinking away. She knew she ought to go after them — and most importantly, after Whyte — but she didn't have the heart. Cole was all that mattered.

"We'll have our way," Whyte shouted as he backed away down the alley. "The pure shall overcome."

The pure shall run like rabbits, Janna wanted to taunt, but she was too busy rushing to Cole. She'd have to fight the rogues another day. Now, all that mattered was her mate.

She whined and circled him, again and again. He swayed on his feet and wagged his tail limply, then wobbled and crumpled to the ground.

Cole, Cole, Cole, she murmured, licking him clean. But God, there was a lot of blood. *Cole...*

Janna, came the weak reply.

She circled around and faced him, nose-to-nose, and studied his eyes. Storm-cloud eyes lit with a thousand lightning sparks. Was that her Cole in there, or was he lost to her forever?

Mate, he mumbled in that gritty wolf voice. He sniffed her closely, just like a wolf would, and her heart sank. Had the beast driven the man out entirely?

Are you... ? Are you... ? she stammered.

109

Cole blinked a few times then cocked his head. *Holy shit, Janna.* He stared. *You're a wolf.*

She could have screamed in relief, because that voice was all Cole.

Yeah, well... she managed a shaky reply. *You're a wolf, too.*

He shook his body meekly, as if to rid himself of the fur, then shoved his head closer. *Are you okay?*

I'm good, she sighed, settling around his body. *Real good.*

The two of them huddled in the littered alley, but all she registered was his heat, his musky, wolf-plus-cowboy scent. A scent she could happily inhale for a long, long time...

Um, Janna... Cole said, looking suddenly lost.

She nestled closer to him. *Let me explain...*

Explain? He shook his head and immediately flicked his eyes to his flopping ears, looking startled. *That might take a while.*

How about a lifetime? she whispered, right in his ear. *Would that do?*

Um... In my regular body or like this?

Her lips curled in a wolf grin. *Your choice, cowboy. Your choice.*

His taut frame seemed to loosen slightly at that, and he nuzzled her. She nuzzled back, and she just might have started humming with pleasure if it hadn't been for the sound of rushing steps at the end of the alley. Janna jumped to her feet and Cole did, too, both of them growling at three looming shadows.

She exhaled a second later, though Cole went right on growling until she called out to her sister in her mind.

Jess!

Cole's angry rumble broke off. *That's Jess?* Then his hackles rose anew as he spotted the two giant grizzlies lumbering up behind Jess.

One step closer and you'll regret it, Cole's snarl warned, though the bears were nearly twice his size.

Janna brushed against his side and stepped forward before anyone tore anyone's throat out. *Simon! Soren!*

Cole's head snapped toward hers. *You're kidding.*

She shook her head. *Not kidding.*

The lights of a squad car appeared behind them, and Janna called out in relief. *Kyle!* The shifter cop from Twin Moon pack would know just how to clean up any evidence of a shifter fight.

He's a wolf, too, she explained to the man at her side.

Cole stared at her, wild-eyed. *Don't tell me the rest of the customers in the saloon can turn into animals.*

Just a few...

A few? Cole didn't look convinced.

Janna, you okay? Simon rumbled.

Yeah, you okay? Soren echoed in his gritty, bear voice.

I'm fine. She looked around the alley and gulped, thinking how close a call it had been.

Jesus, what happened? Jess asked.

And who the hell is this? Simon demanded.

Soren stood behind him, baring his teeth at Cole.

This, she said, stepping between them, *is Cole.*

Cole? Jess peeped.

Simon pulled back. *Holy...*

...Shit, Soren finished.

Yeah, that about summed up her evening. But, hell, she'd gone this far; she wasn't backing down now.

Cole. She nodded fiercely. *My mate. My destined mate.*

Cole growled at her side, echoing the sentiment. *Mate. My destined mate.*

Epilogue

One month later. . .

Sunlight stretched in through the long, arched windows, and although Cole's eyes were closed, he could feel the warmth on his bare skin. His chest rose and fell under the light weight of Janna's arm, looped over him, and he sighed a little.

Another beautiful morning, another beautiful day. It was late — too late for any self-respecting cowboy to be waking up, but he and Janna had been out running for most of the previous night.

The door separating them from the rest of the apartment above the Blue Moon Saloon was closed, but the sound of footsteps and two voices carried from down the hall.

"Those two still catching up on sleep?" Simon chuckled.

Jessica shushed him. "As if you're any better, bear."

Cole rolled to face Janna, still asleep at his side, and ran a finger gently along her cheek. Truthfully, he was still catching up on a lot of things. Like the fact that he could shift back and forth between human and wolf forms, and that Janna could, too.

It had been a crazy couple of weeks. Janna hadn't left his side the entire time, seeing him through what she called the Change. He'd survived a week of fever and wracking pain after the night of his first shift, and there'd been times when he'd felt one howl away from insanity. But her voice and touch always pulled him back, and he'd come out the other side of the tunnel to a place brighter and sunnier than he'd ever been before. That peaceful mountain meadow was part of his world now, all the time.

113

Without Janna, he never would have made it. She helped his two sides work together as partners instead of rivals. The wolf was his ally, and Janna's, too. All those terrible images he'd seen weren't his wolf hurting Janna, but a foreshadowing of the rogues. The rogues his wolf had saved her from.

Told you so, the voice yawned inside.

It still took some getting used to, even now that the worst had passed. Sometimes, being a wolf came naturally, as it had that night of the rogue attack, when he needed it most. All he'd had to do was turn his brain off and trust the wolf to coordinate four feet, a hell of a lot of sharp claws, and a really, really startling set of teeth.

It was like Janna said all the times they'd gone out in the forest since then to practice *wolf stuff,* as she so casually called shifting and howling and shagging on four feet. *Just follow your instincts.*

The first time she'd said that, she'd been standing in the light of the pale, waning moon, lit up like a goddess of the night. Janna the wolf, as sleek and sweet and spunky as she was in human form.

Instinct, huh? he couldn't resist shooting back. *You know what instinct is telling me to do right now?*

Instinct had led him right through their first round of sex, wolf-style. The feverish, satisfied sounds Janna made told him he'd done that pretty well, too. And a couple of nights later, when they'd been two human lovers going at it in bed, instinct had told him just how and when to deliver the mating bite. The high that came with it still made him tingle, even want to roar.

Mine! My mate!

When he overthought things, though, he still made for a clumsy canine. Scratching an ear with his back foot was a trick he hadn't quite mastered yet, and Janna collapsed into laughter every time he fell trying it. Which was okay because she said it was cute, and she always made it up to him with a long, wolf lick or a nuzzling session that could go on and on and on.

"Mmm," she sighed dreamily beside him. "Cole..."

114

Oops. He'd only meant to touch her, but it had turned into another nuzzle.

"Can't help it," he murmured. "Not with my mate."

That was another thing that gave him a ridiculous sense of pride. Saying those two words. *My mate.* When Janna had said it that night in the alley, he'd understood the true meaning in his bones, in his soul. Mate.

His, forever. He leaned closer and whispered it in her ear.

Her naked body arched, stretched, and settled down again under his touch.

"Mmm," she mumbled. "Nice way to wake up."

It was a nice way to wake up. Slowly. Sober. A little sore from shifting, but just enough to feel settled and peaceful inside.

The place was part of it, too. After a couple of weeks going back and forth between his place and hers, they'd settled into hers, which meant the three rooms in their own little wing at the back of the apartment over the saloon. Soren had the first room at the top of the stairs. Jessica and Simon had the suite of rooms above the café. All of it was interconnected by a hallway with just enough sharp turns in it to give everyone their own space. The apartment really needed a second bathroom and a lot of fixing up, but overall, it was good. Really good.

The first week had been a little awkward, dealing with housemates who could shift into deadly grizzlies or wolves at will, but once they'd all staked out their respective territories, he'd been accepted as if he'd been there from the very start. The bear brothers called their funny little rooming situation a clan, while Janna and Jessica insisted on calling it a pack. Either way, Cole liked it. A lot. In a way, he'd been part of a pack all his life: growing up with a lot of siblings, then working the bull-riding circuit, when he'd traveled and roomed with his brothers or buddies. It was only during those lost, empty couple of months before he met Janna that he'd been alone, and that hadn't suited him at all.

Janna slid a hand up and down his belly, making him hum.

"Watch it, lady."

"Not up for a little fun?" she teased. Just her voice was a temptation, never mind the warm curves begging to be touched.

He snorted and scooped her into his arms. "Fun is riding. Dancing. Having a tail." He grinned, then pressed his lips to hers. "This is more than fun."

He wasn't sure what the right word was, but it had to be made up of more than three little letters and one short syllable. What he had with Janna... Yeah, a hell of a lot more than fun.

He kissed his way over to her ear, then started down her chest, relishing the way she sighed and rose under his touch. The way her skin heated made him go hard, and the scent of her arousal filled the room, driving him wild.

"Yes..." she murmured, guiding his head lower.

He was an inch south of her belly button and headed for heaven when a knock came at the door.

"Janna! Cole!"

"Nuh-uh," Janna muttered. "Not answering that. So not answering that." She threaded her fingers into his hair, coaxing him along.

The scar of the mating bite she'd left on his neck tingled, making his whole body hot.

"Janna!" Soren called in his deep, authoritative voice.

Cole broke away. Soren was the alpha of the pack. Even if Janna treated him as more of an older brother than almighty ruler, Cole knew all about hierarchy and order. He might be top dog when it came to things like bulls, but under this roof, Soren was boss, and Cole sure as hell wasn't going to get on the bear's bad side. Being the only unmated shifter in the clan could make a guy grouchy — especially given that Soren had lost his destined mate in a fire. Cole didn't even want to think about how bad that would be, so, yeah, he always cut the guy some slack.

"Later," Cole whispered into her belly button. "I promise this will be twice as good later."

"Not possible," Janna grumbled.

"Come on!" Soren called. "Jess wants everyone downstairs, now."

"Is it eleven o'clock already?" Janna glared at the clock.

Cole slid along her body, slowly sitting up. "Come on, it's her big day." He turned his head and called to Soren, "Be right there."

"Opening day is tomorrow," Janna sighed. "Couldn't we toast the café opening then?"

"She's already pushed it back two weeks for us."

"Get moving, already," Soren called from the other side of the door.

Janna grumbled a little longer, but she brightened with each layer of clothing she slipped on and each step she bounced down on her way to the ground floor.

"Quarter Moon Café," he chuckled. "I love the name of the new place."

They stepped out the back door of the saloon and circled around into the café next door.

"Hello?" Janna called.

"We're out front," Jess called.

Janna dragged him past the enticing scent of the muffins to the airy front room of the café, where everyone was gathered. Jess brushed the crumbs off Simon's face, looking ridiculously happy. Tina Hawthorne was there, too, with her mate, Rick Rivera, the wolf shifter who owned the property adjoining Twin Moon Ranch.

"Ready to start work soon?" Rick asked as Cole shook his hand. Rick, his new boss, because Cole had scored the perfect job at Seymour Ranch. "We're desperate for help with those new bulls we got in."

Cole grinned. He'd been by Seymour Ranch to teach Rick's ranch hands how to handle the new stock and had immediately been offered a job. The new cattle could turn great profits as organic beef, but they'd been causing the ranch hands hell ever since they'd arrived.

"Can't wait," he said, grinning from ear to ear.

It was true. He couldn't wait to start. His month of settling into his new skin was almost up, and it was time to earn an honest wage again. He'd been helping Rosalind transition to a new stable hand. Two, in fact — a very capable, very eager brother-sister team who hailed from a wolf pack up in Colorado. Not that Rosalind knew about the wolf part.

The only aspect of the new setup he didn't like would be the hours of separation from Janna, but they'd get through that, too.

"Okay, everybody. Here we go," Jessica cleared her throat and handed him a champagne flute. "To the Quarter Moon Café."

Everyone raised their glasses and watched Jessica's eyes shine at the idea of a dream come true. It was exactly the same way Janna's eyes shone at him — and probably the way his eyes glowed right back at his mate.

"To the Quarter Moon Café," everyone echoed with a hearty cheer.

"To a great manager." Tina nodded to Jess.

"To lots more muffins," Simon added.

"To more working hours," Janna chimed in, wearing a wry smile. Other than worrying about Victor Whyte, the rogue leader who'd slipped away, the only thing the Blue Moon clan had to fret about was finding enough help to run both the saloon and the café.

Tina pinched her lips together. "I found someone to help here all next week. After that... Well, I'm working on it."

Rick pulled Tina into his side, and Cole was tempted to do the same with Janna. He let his eyes drift across the cheery faces. Everyone working together, pulling together, helping each other along. The way it should be.

A figure walked by the front doors then pulled up short, and he smiled. Getting people to try out the new café wouldn't be hard, not with Jessica's cooking and Janna's knack for pulling customers in.

He looked more closely and realized the woman outside wasn't looking at the colorful tables and chairs he'd helped paint. She wasn't studying the menu Jessica had posted in the window, either. She seemed lost and weary. Except for the swell of an unmissable baby bump, the woman was thin. Too thin. She stood in the bright sunlight, teetered on her feet, and—

Whoa! Cole ran to the sidewalk just in time to get an arm around her before she crashed to the ground.

"Whoa there. You all right?"

She sure didn't look all right, so he steered her into the café despite her mumbled protests.

"Oh, you poor thing," Jessica cooed, guiding the stranger in.

Janna and Tina dashed in to help, too, and as they took over, he caught a glimpse of wicked burn scars running down the woman's arm.

"Rick, get her a cushion."

"Get her a glass of water, too," Jess said, kneeling by the woman.

"I'm fine," the woman insisted, but her voice was weak and uncertain. "Just need a minute. . . "

She needed about six weeks, Cole figured, until that baby was ready to take on the world. The woman was gaunt, but her belly was stretched with what had to be seven or eight months of baby. For a moment, he panicked, thinking she might be in early labor.

The woman puffed once or twice and sat straighter. "I'm fine," she repeated, a little more insistently.

The curtain of her hair fell back, and Soren froze in front of her, holding a glass in midair.

"Soren!" Janna chided.

"Soren?" the newcomer whispered.

"Sarah," he whispered, barely above the sound of his breath.

For a moment, everyone stood still. Time stood still, and Cole's mind whirled. Janna had explained about Soren being in love with a human from back home in Montana. A girl named Sarah who'd died in a fire. . .

One look at the way Soren and the woman stared at each other told him this was that Sarah. So she hadn't died in that fire. She was alive. Alive and expecting a baby. . .

119

His mind spun through the math. According to Janna, the fire happened seven months ago and Soren had been away a few months before that. Which meant that baby had to have been conceived sometime after Soren left.

Oh, shit.

The woman's hand dropped to her rounded belly, and when Soren's eyes followed, the glass slipped out of his hand and shattered on the floor.

The woman's eyes remained dry, but her expression wept with something like, *Let me explain.*

Before the splinters came to rest on the new linoleum floor, Soren wheeled and strode out of the room. Not a word. Not a backward glance. Not a sign of emotion. But the air around him wavered with sorrow and doubt.

"Soren!" Janna called sharply, but the bear shifter was gone.

Cole's eyes met Janna's and he gulped. They'd found their happiness — but Soren... God, how would he ever find his?

Sneak Peek: Redemption

True love is about forgiveness, not pride.

Bear shifter Soren Voss lives and breathes for the new clan he leads as alpha. It's all he has left after the rogue ambush that murdered the woman he loved — the woman he swears he'll always love, even if it's only in his dreams. But the day his dream comes true is also the start of a nightmare, because his destined mate may no longer be his and his alone. Is it fate's way of torturing him or his last chance at redemption?

Sarah Boone narrowly escaped the inferno that claimed her family and her home. For months now, she's been on the run with a secret that will soon be impossible to hide. But the clock is ticking, and she needs a place to settle down soon. She never expected to find the love of her life running a funky little place called the Blue Moon Saloon. He's darker and more dangerous than ever, but somehow more vulnerable, too. Does she have it in her to be the woman her world-weary warrior needs most of all?

Don't miss the action, passion, or romance. Get your copy of REDEMPTION today! Available as ebook, paperback, and audiobook.

Books by Anna Lowe

Blue Moon Saloon

Perfection (a short story prequel)

Damnation (Book 1)

Temptation (Book 2)

Redemption (Book 3)

Salvation (Book 4)

Deception (Book 5)

Celebration (a holiday treat)

Aloha Shifters - Jewels of the Heart

Lure of the Dragon (Book 1)

Lure of the Wolf (Book 2)

Lure of the Bear (Book 3)

Lure of the Tiger (Book 4)

Love of the Dragon (Book 5)

Lure of the Fox (Book 6)

Aloha Shifters - Pearls of Desire

Rebel Dragon (Book 1)

Rebel Bear (Book 2)

Rebel Lion (Book 3)

Rebel Wolf (Book 4)

Rebel Heart (A prequel to Book 5)

Rebel Alpha (Book 5)

Fire Maidens - Billionaires & Bodyguards

Fire Maidens: Paris (Book 1)

Fire Maidens: London (Book 2)

Fire Maidens: Rome (Book 3)

Fire Maidens: Portugal (Book 4)

Fire Maidens: Ireland (Book 5)

The Wolves of Twin Moon Ranch

Desert Hunt (the Prequel)

Desert Moon (Book 1)

Desert Blood (Book 2)

Desert Fate (Book 3)

Desert Heart (Book 4)

Desert Rose (Book 5)

Desert Roots (Book 6)

Desert Yule (a short story)

Desert Wolf: Complete Collection (Four short stories)

Sasquatch Surprise (a Twin Moon spin-off story)

Shifters in Vegas

Paranormal romance with a zany twist

Gambling on Trouble

Gambling on Her Dragon

Gambling on Her Bear

Serendipity Adventure Romance

Off the Charts

Uncharted

Entangled

Windswept

Adrift

Travel Romance

Veiled Fantasies

Island Fantasies

visit www.annalowebooks.com

About the Author

USA Today and Amazon bestselling author Anna Lowe loves putting the "hero" back into heroine and letting location ignite a passionate romance. She likes a heroine who is independent, intelligent, and imperfect – a woman who is doing just fine on her own. But give the heroine a good man – not to mention a chance to overcome her own inhibitions – and she'll never turn down the chance for adventure, nor shy away from danger.

Anna loves dogs, sports, and travel – and letting those inspire her fiction. On any given weekend, you might find her hiking in the mountains or hunched over her laptop, working on her latest story. Either way, the day will end with a chunk of dark chocolate and a good read.

Visit AnnaLoweBooks.com

Printed in Great Britain
by Amazon